Longarm had the woman's pretty bare leg right next to his face, and it occurred to him that Lucy Ortega had lovely calves.

"There," he said. "Try that."

"Perfect," she said. And Lucy suddenly jammed her foot back into the stirrup and kicked him in the face.

"Ya!" she cried, whirling the mare around, grabbing Longarm's own horse by the reins, and making a break for it down the center of the street.

Longarm swore and clutched at his bleeding nose. Maybe Lucy Ortega had broken it, but there was no time to find out—because she was disappearing in one hell of a big cloud of dust . . .

DON'T MISS THESE
ALL-ACTION WESTERN SERIES
FROM THE BERKLEY PUBLISHING GROUP

THE GUNSMITH by J. R. Roberts
> Clint Adams was a legend among lawmen, outlaws, and ladies. They called him . . . the Gunsmith.

LONGARM by Tabor Evans
> The popular long-running series about U.S. Deputy Marshal Long—his life, his loves, his fight for justice.

LONE STAR by Wesley Ellis
> The blazing adventures of Jessica Starbuck and the martial arts master, Ki. Over eight million copies in print.

SLOCUM by Jake Logan
> Today's longest-running action Western. John Slocum rides a deadly trail of hot blood and cold steel.

TABOR EVANS

LONGARM

AND THE YUMA PRISON GIRLS

JOVE BOOKS, NEW YORK

LONGARM AND THE YUMA PRISON GIRLS

A Jove Book / published by arrangement with
the author

PRINTING HISTORY
Jove edition / March 1995

All rights reserved.
Copyright © 1995 by Jove Publications, Inc.
This book may not be reproduced in whole
or in part, by mimeograph or any other means,
without permission. For information address:
The Berkley Publishing Group, 200 Madison Avenue,
New York, New York 10016.

ISBN: 0-515-11569-X

A JOVE BOOK®
Jove Books are published by The Berkley Publishing Group,
200 Madison Avenue, New York, New York 10016.
JOVE and the "J" design are trademarks
belonging to Jove Publications, Inc.

PRINTED IN THE UNITED STATES OF AMERICA

10 9 8 7 6 5 4 3 2 1

LONGARM

AND THE
YUMA PRISON GIRLS

Chapter 1

"Come in, come in!" United States Marshal Billy Vail called from behind his huge and cluttered desk. "I've been expecting you."

Custis Long removed his Stetson, beat a cloud of trail dust from his clothes, and entered from the outer office. To Billy he looked the very picture of a frontier lawman. Custis was a big man, just over six-two and broad-shouldered, with a deeply tanned face and gunmetal gray eyes. He wore a handlebar mustache, fashionably curled at the tips, and on his hip was a well-used double-action Colt Model T. caliber .44-40. Custis always looked formidable, but today even more than usual as he slouched into a chair, removed a nickel cheroot from his pocket, and jammed it into his mouth.

"Want a light?" Billy offered.

"Nope, prefer to chew the damned things now, I expect you know that, Billy."

"Sure." Billy regarded his best marshal with some concern. "You look worn down, Custis. This last assignment was pretty tough, huh?"

"Damn right it was," Custis growled around his cigar. "You told me to find and arrest Trace Hollaway. But what you *didn't* tell me was that he had a whole pack of brothers that were every bit as mean and trigger-happy as he was."

"The brothers gave you trouble?" Billy asked.

"Sure they did! I caught Trace in Central City humpin' a whore and I smacked him on the head with my six-gun. Hauled his naked ass out the second floor of the whorehouse and was lashing him across the back of my packhorse when those ornery brothers came rushing up to help."

Billy leaned forward in his chair. "I expect that was quite a fight, huh?"

"You damn sure betcha it was. I tried to explain that I had a warrant for Trace's arrest and was doing everything legal, but they wouldn't listen. One of the fools went for his gun and I had to kill him, then I shot the rest of 'em all to pieces. It was a real mess."

"How many did you kill?"

"Four," Longarm spat. "Well, three, actually. One lived, but he'll be a gimpy sonofabitch for the rest of his life. My last bullet caught him in the hip. I expect he won't be sending me any love letters."

Longarm's eyebrows forked downward and he jabbed a finger at his boss. "Billy, why didn't you tell me that Trace had four meaner-than-snakes brothers?"

"I thought they were still hiding out in Wyoming," Billy explained. "There was a stagecoach robbery up there and the four were identified."

"Well," Longarm said after a moment, "it's clear that

they came back to Colorado. It would have helped me some to have known about 'em. That kind of thing can get a man killed."

"It sounds as if it did."

"Gawdammit, I meant *me*," Longarm snapped. "If you knew about those other four, I should have had some backup."

"I apologize," Billy said with a very benign and disarming smile.

"You do?" Longarm leaned back in his chair. He'd worked for Billy Vail a good many years now, and while this wasn't the man's first apology, it was one of a very few.

"Yes," Billy said in complete agreement. "And I mean to put your name in for a Governor's Commendation as soon as I get your written report. Those four brothers were wanted for stage and train robberies in at least three states, including this one."

Longarm actually smiled. "Any chance of picking up a little reward money?"

"Of course not! You know better than that. A reward doesn't come with your job."

"A job," Longarm groused, "that is long on commendations but damned short of cash."

Billy chuckled as he leaned back in his big, soft chair and steepled his short, pudgy fingers. In contrast to Longarm, he was round and jovial-looking, although that was quite deceptive. Billy had a very impressive record from his years of working as a deputy marshal out in the field. He was so harmless-looking that he always managed to lull his opponents into a false sense of security before making his move. Billy Vail had courage, and there was muscle under that thick layer of flab.

Now Billy's eyes twinkled. He plucked a cigar from

an open box, but replaced it after a moment's consideration and returned his attention to the deputy marshal. "I've another assignment waiting for you, Longarm."

"Oh, no!" Longarm stopped chewing his cigar. "You told me that I could have a week off after I brought Trace in for sentencing and that's what I mean to do, take a full week off."

"And you richly deserve that week and much more!" Billy exclaimed, nodding his head so emphatically that his double chins quivered. "But this is a *special* assignment, my friend! Very special."

"I don't care if it's to escort the Queen of England! I need a rest, Billy. I haven't even had time to spend my last six months worth of government paychecks."

"Then you should save them," Billy said earnestly. "You know, field work is for young men. And how old are you, Custis?"

"You know damn good and well how old I am," Longarm spat. "I'm old enough to be seasoned and still plenty young and quick enough to handle whatever trouble comes in my direction."

"Yes, yes, of course," Billy said. "I know that, but in a few more years . . . well, you really ought to begin a savings plan now, Custis. I'm enrolled in one. Most of the senior men in our department are."

Longarm groaned. "Billy, just give me that week off and we can talk about all this later," he said, pushing himself wearily to his feet.

Billy also came to his feet. He was dressed in a black, pin-stripped suit, with a white shirt with starched collar and a wine-colored tie. He looked quite natty as he skirted his massive mahogany desk and reached up to lay a pudgy hand on Longarm's shoulder.

"Look, I tell you what I'm going to do."

4

"Oh, no," Longarm said, brushing Billy's hand aside and confronting the man. "Don't give me any of that bullshit of yours, Billy. What you are going to do is to give me the full week of paid vacation time that you've been promising for the last two years."

"I'm going to do that," Billy persisted, "and *more.*"

Longarm's voice dropped. "You are?"

"Sure! Actually, I'm going to give you *two* weeks of paid vacation."

"Really?" Longarm allowed himself to smile. "If I had two weeks, I'd go to St. Louis and then maybe take a riverboat down to New Orleans."

"Hell," Billy chuckled, "that kind of trip would take you two *months!* And even then I'd be lucky if I got you back in one piece. Those riverboats are pretty wild and dangerous."

"I've been on 'em," Longarm said. "And I can handle whatever comes my way."

"I know that full well," Billy said, returning to his chair. "Sit down and let me tell you exactly what you'll have to do in order to earn that extra week of *paid* vacation."

Despite his better judgment, Longarm returned to his seat. He stretched his long legs out and laced his hands behind his head. He would take whatever Billy said with a heavy measure of skepticism. "All right, Billy, but I know you well enough to recognize a trap when I'm about to be snared."

"This is no trap," Billy promised. "In fact, most any deputy marshal in this office would crawl over broken glass to have this assignment."

"Sure," Longarm drawled, not believing a word Billy said. "Let's hear it."

Billy had a flair for the dramatic and he liked to draw

5

out anything suspenseful, so he picked up a cigar again, contemplated it for several long moments, then replaced it in his open box. "Custis, there is a very special prisoner that needs to be delivered to the Arizona Territorial Prison at Yuma."

"Oh, kee-rist!" Longarm said, jumping to his feet. "That's a hellhole! And even to get there is a real sonofabitch. Don't you know that the Apache are raisin' hell again down in that part of the country?"

"Crook has all but put them under his authority," Billy said with a smile.

"How come this prisoner has to be transported to Yuma, of all places? Why can't he just be tried here?"

"First of all," Billy explained patiently, "the prisoner has committed a crime in the Arizona Territory, with which we have a reciprocal agreement for prisoner exchanges. That means that we agree to give up our prisoners and transport them to Arizona and they agree to hand over any prisoners who have committed federal felonies here in Colorado. So you see, Custis, it works both ways."

"Yeah," Longarm said, "but the rub is that some poor deputy like me has to transport them to hell and back."

"I'm sorry," Billy said, not looking a bit sorry, "but I've given this matter some very serious consideration and you are definitely the best man for the job. In fact, you're the only one that I have complete confidence in regarding this particular prisoner."

"Is this prisoner a one-man army?"

Marshal Billy Vail had a cherubic face and a boyish grin that often won him an argument, and he used it now. "Actually, the *he* is a *she*."

Longarm collapsed into his chair. "The prisoner is a woman?"

"That's right," Billy said. "And she is quite young and beautiful."

"Well, hell," Longarm blurted out in confusion. "Why do you want *me?*"

"Because you *know* all the tricks that a beautiful woman will use on a man to get her way. And this woman is clever as a fox. Why, if I gave her over to the care and protection of a younger man, she'd have him wrapped around her little finger before they got beyond the city line. And she'd have him helping her escape before they were out of Colorado."

"Maybe you aren't giving your men enough credit."

"Oh," Billy said, "I don't mean to belittle our newer deputy marshals. We've some very good ones. But this job definitely needs a man like you who is well seasoned. Someone who has enough experience and maturity to handle bad women."

"How do you know I have that?"

"Come on, Longarm. There isn't a decent woman in Denver safe from your line of malarkey."

"Pure poppycock!" Longarm snorted. "I've never had anything to do with married women, or those that were fat, old, or ugly."

"How gentlemanly of you," Billy said, voice now dripping with sarcasm.

"Who is this woman that you want me to take to Yuma?"

"You'd know the answer to that if you'd read yesterday's newspaper," Billy said. "Her picture was even on the front page. Want to see it?"

"No," Longarm said, "I'd rather take one week vacation starting today and forget about this woman and about the territorial prison at Yuma."

Billy's smile melted. "Well, Deputy, I'm afraid that

you do not have that choice. I need you to take Mrs. Lucy Ortega to Yuma as quickly as possible, stopping off at the town marshal's office in Prescott."

"Why the stop?"

"There's some question of exactly how Mrs. Ortega murdered her husband and where she hid the body. I'm hoping that the boys in Prescott will have filled in some of the pieces of this puzzle so that, by the time you get Mrs. Ortega to Yuma, there is a clear-cut case against her."

"You mean, there's some doubt if she killed her husband?"

"Not much of one," Billy said. "Just yesterday we caught Mrs. Ortega trying to board the train north to Cheyenne. She'd bought a transfer ticket to Omaha, and would have vanished into the East if we hadn't gotten a little lucky."

"I see," Longarm said. "Where's that newspaper with her picture on the front page?"

Billy reached down into his desk and opened the bottom drawer. He drew the newspaper out, unfolded it, and turned it around so that Longarm could see Lucy Ortega.

"Beautiful, isn't she," Billy said, craning his neck to see the picture he had already stared at longer than he cared to admit.

"Quite," Longarm agreed. "For a woman named Ortega, she doesn't look Mexican or Spanish."

"That's because she isn't. She's Irish. But her husband was a very wealthy Spaniard, son of a grandee or some such thing. Lucy was educated at an exclusive ladies school in the East. She went west, met this Spanish nobleman, and they were married. They were on their ranch in Prescott when they got into a loud argument and she killed him, then vanished. It was just luck that we snared her at our train station."

Longarm stared at the picture. Lucy Ortega was a real beauty, with long, dark, and lustrous hair. Her face was an oval, and Longarm could see that the picture must have been taken at her wedding because of her dress. She appeared as radiant as expected for a virgin bride.

"What kind of evidence is there against this woman?"

"There were witnesses," Billy explained. "Three of them that said they were just outside the room when they heard Mrs. Ortega shoot her husband during a violent quarrel."

"Heard?"

"That's right. They didn't actually see the shooting."

Longarm shook his head. "To tell you the truth, Billy, Mrs. Ortega sure doesn't look like a cold-blooded murderess to me."

"Do beautiful young women ever look like killers?" Billy asked softly.

"No," Longarm admitted. "I suppose not." He tore his eyes from the picture. "Is there anything else that you have to tell me about this miserable job?"

"Yes, I'm afraid so. This is going to be a prisoner exchange."

"A what?"

"A prisoner exchange," Billy repeated. "You'll be bringing back some female prisoners from Yuma."

"Damnation!" Longarm swore. "How many?"

"I'm not sure," Billy said, trying to smile. "Probably only a few, no more than . . . oh, at last count, a dozen."

"Jezus, Billy! A dozen women inmates! I quit!"

Longarm jumped for the door, but Billy called out,

"Wait. I've been assured that you'll be given more than enough help by the Arizona Territory officials. Please, be reasonable and hear me out, Custis. That's all I'm asking. Hear me out."

Longarm hauled up at the door and turned around. "When you say 'help,' how much and who?"

"I can't tell you for sure. I can promise you, however, that the Arizona Territory is footing the bill for a prison wagon in addition to a couple of their own lawmen who will accompany you and the female inmates back to Denver."

"Great," Longarm said with complete disgust. "I'm supposed to haul a wagonful of wicked women clean across a thousand miles of burning sand and sage, then over a mountain range. Are you folks out of your minds!"

"Perhaps," Billy confessed, "but I have every confidence that you'll do just fine."

"Easy for you to say," Longarm growled.

"All right. I admit that this is not going to be entirely pleasant. That's why I've gotten permission to reward you with *two full weeks* of paid vacation beginning on the very day that you return."

"A month," Longarm said between clenched teeth.

"I beg your pardon?"

"This is going to be a murderous job and you know it, Billy. I want a full month."

"Out of the question!"

"I have it coming!" Longarm stood up and he was angry. "Look at me, dammit! I'm whipped. I haven't had a single day off in over a year! I'm getting burned out and I'm just about ready to quit."

"You wouldn't!"

"I would," Longarm said, his voice hard-edged. "This

Central City job was close, Billy. Real close. You sent me into a hornet's nest with all them brothers, and it was only luck that kept me from getting gunned down."

"It wasn't just luck," Billy argued. "A man like you makes his own luck."

"Maybe, but it was close," Longarm said. "Now what's it to be? Do I get a month's vacation with pay or am I supposed to turn in my badge?"

Billy stood up and began to pace back and forth between his desk and the back wall. Longarm just waited. He figured he had Billy over a barrel and he wasn't about to let him slip off the hook.

"I'll tell you what, Custis. "I *might* be able to get you three weeks. Might. How would that be?"

"Three weeks? All right," Longarm said after a few moments of hard deliberation. "But when I get back, if that three weeks isn't approved, I'm handing over my badge. Do you understand me?"

"Of course," Billy said, looking slightly offended. "I don't see how you could make it any clearer."

"Good," Longarm said. "Now, is there anything else I should know about this Mrs. Lucy Ortega that you've neglected to tell me? Anything at all?"

"No," Billy said, pursing his lips in concentration. "I think that it's all pretty well spelled out. She's young, beautiful, smart, and probably devious. You'll need to be on constant guard. She'll probably try to win your favor, playing to your manliness. But you can't let yourself get personally involved. Consider her to be like . . . like a coral snake."

"A coral snake?"

"Yes," Billy said, clearly pleased with the analogy, "because they are very beautiful but also very deadly."

11

"I'll try," Longarm said, eyes dropping back to the newspaper picture.

"Do better than *try,* Longarm. Do much better or you will most certainly be poisoned."

Longarm scowled, and then turned on his heel and went back to the door.

"Oh, Custis?"

"Yeah?"

"I forgot to ask. Did you put in an expense sheet on that Hollaway business?"

"Not yet. Hell, Billy, I just got back into town a few minutes ago, for crying out loud."

"They're waiting in our financial department," Billy said, his blue eyes dropping to regard a memorandum on his desk. "And they are not too happy with the way you tallied up the expenses for your last assignment. You need to keep receipts and better records."

Longarm's eyes widened and his lips pulled back from his teeth. "I'll talk to them in the financial department," he growled, "and I'll enjoy the looks on their faces when I tell those paper-pushers where I'm going to deposit my receipts and records from this last trip."

Longarm slammed out of the door and left Billy Vail chuckling.

Chapter 2

"She's all yours, Deputy Long," the jail guard said, stepping aside so that Longarm could get his prisoner.

Lucy Ortega was not at her best. Her hair was tangled and her dress soiled and torn, indicating to Longarm that she had probably resisted arrest. The cell she occupied was dank and dingy and the light poor, but Longarm could still see that Mrs. Ortega was a beautiful woman. Her skin was flawless and her hair was either black or a very deep mahogany brown. She was tall, at least five-foot-ten, with strong features.

"Good afternoon, Mrs. Ortega," Longarm said by the way of introduction. "My name is Deputy Marshal Custis Long and I've been assigned to escort you to Yuma."

Lucy sat on a hard metal bench that also served as a bed. She glared at Longarm without saying anything, and did not even attempt to come to her feet.

"I guess you don't have much in the way of belongings," Longarm said, looking around the jail cell and seeing nothing. "The bailiff has your handbag and the coat you were wearing when you were arrested. We might as well go."

Lucy just glared at him.

"Ma'am," Longarm said, stepping closer. "I want you to know that I'm not real happy about going to Yuma either. Fact of the matter is, Yuma is one of my least favorite places. But you're part of a prisoner swap and neither one of us has any choice about going."

"Go away," she ordered in a deep, harsh voice. "Just get out of here, Marshal, and neither one of us will get hurt."

Longarm frowned. He had handled women prisoners before, but had never felt very comfortable doing so. He decided to be more firm with this woman. "Now, Mrs. Ortega, I . . ."

"Lucy! My husband is dead and my name is Lucy."

"Sure," Longarm replied, nodding his head and wondering if Lucy was a little crazy. "I don't care what I call you. But we do have to go to Yuma."

"I'm not going back to Arizona," she said in a flat, no-compromise tone of voice.

"You got that wrong," Longarm told her. "I've been ordered to take you to Yuma via Prescott."

Her hard expression changed and she came to her feet. "We're going to Prescott?"

"Yes," he said, "something about witnesses and evidence. I don't know, but I expect someone will be waiting to tell us everything we need to know. Anyway, we've got to get started while the day is still young. It's a long ride to Prescott, even a longer one to Yuma."

"No train or stagecoach?" she asked.

14

"Nope," Longarm said. "The way we're traveling, they would take us far afield. I've rented us a pair of good saddle horses."

Longarm stared at the woman. "You can ride a horse, can't you?"

"Of course," she said.

"Then let's go, Miss . . . I mean Lucy."

She thought about that for a moment, as if going or staying was her decision alone, then made up her mind. With a nod of her head, she came towards him, forcing Longarm to back out of the cell.

"Now, Lucy," he said, removing a set of handcuffs from his belt, "I'm afraid that I'm going to have to ask you to wear these."

She came right up to him and said, "You're afraid of me?"

"No, of course not!" He cleared his throat. "It's just federal regulations that all prisoners wear handcuffs. If you were a man, I'd also slap a pair of leg irons on you, but . . ."

She stuck out her wrists and squeezed them together. "Go ahead, put them on and then put on the leg irons."

"Won't need to do the latter," Longarm said, handcuffing her.

"No," she insisted, reaching down with her manacled wrists and tugging up her dress to the knee as she thrust a shapely calf forward. "Put them on!"

"I didn't even bring the damned things," he said, losing patience. "Now just follow me."

Longarm wouldn't have turned his back, even on a woman prisoner, except that she had riled him and he wanted to show her that he was not in the least bit afraid of her hurting him or trying to escape. He led her to

15

the jail officer's desk, where Lucy Ortega collected her handbag and meager belongings, then escorted her out of the jail and into the street.

"Ready to ride?" he said, untying their waiting horses.

"It would help if I had a riding skirt," she told him. "How am I supposed to ride in a full dress with a petticoat?"

"Hike it up," he said, grabbing Lucy by the waist and lifting her up into the saddle with more effort than he'd expected. Lucy Ortega was not a willowy woman. She was full-bodied and strong. Longarm made a mental note to himself to remember that, with a weapon in her hand, Lucy would be quite formidable.

Lucy reached down and gathered up her reins. Longarm looked back over his shoulder and saw several of the jail guards grinning at him.

"You boys see something funny?" he asked in a challenging voice. "Because if you do, why don't you let me in on it so I can grin like a fool too?"

The jail guards disappeared back inside. Longarm climbed onto a tall, rangy sorrel gelding that he called Duke and had used on many occasions.

"What is this mare's name?" Lucy asked.

"I don't know. First time I ever rented her." Longarm studied the pretty roan. "You can call her anything you want."

"I'll call her Strawberry," Lucy said, stroking the mare's sleek neck.

"Good enough," Longarm said, noting how Lucy's hardness melted a little as she stroked the mare's coat. "I can see that you like horses. Are the stirrups long enough?"

"Not really," she said, hiking the dress up to her thighs. "Would you be kind enough to lengthen them?"

16

"Sure," he said, dismounting. "We've got a long ride ahead of us and I'll buy you a riding skirt at the mercantile before we leave town."

She smiled and kicked her feet out of her stirrups. "That would be very kind of you."

Longarm had to unlace the stirrup in order to lengthen it, and that took several minutes. While doing so, he had the woman's pretty bare leg right next to his face, and it occurred to him that Lucy Ortega had lovely calves.

"There," he said. "Try that."

"Perfect," she said.

"One more," he said, moving around the horse to the off stirrup. He quickly unlaced it, and was starting to pull the stirrup down when Lucy suddenly jammed her foot back into the stirrup and kicked him in the face.

"Ya!" she cried, whirling the mare around, grabbing Longarm's own horse by the reins, and making a break for it down the center of the street.

Longarm swore and clutched at his bleeding nose. Maybe Lucy Ortega had broken it, but there was no time to find out because she was disappearing in one hell of a big cloud of dust. Up and down the street people were scattering in an attempt to avoid being run over.

Longarm spotted a horse tied at a hitch rail about twenty yards away and sprinted to it. He tore the reins free, then jumped into the saddle and took off after the woman fugitive. If Lucy had been a man, he would have pulled his six-gun and winged her in the shoulder.

Blood was pouring from his nose as he followed Lucy through town heading due east toward the Kansas plains. Fortunately, the horse he had commandeered was faster than Lucy's mare, and he managed to overtake her about a mile out of town. She was giving it her best try, however, and he had to admire her determination when he finally came abreast of her and grabbed her long reddish-brown hair and nearly jerked her out of the saddle.

"Rein in, damn you!" Longarm shouted. "Rein in!"

But Lucy wasn't about to rein in. She tried to hit him in the nose again, but she was off balance and swinging back over her shoulder, so there was no power in her punches. For his own part, Longarm had had about enough. Lucy Ortega had embarrassed the hell out of him before half of the citizens of Denver, probably broken his nose, and forced him to steal another man's horse.

"That's it!" Longarm stormed as his patience snapped and he dragged Lucy off the back of her running horse.

She hit hard and bounced a good two feet, then rolled over and over. When Longarm finally got the horses stopped, he dismounted and hurried back, sure that maybe the witch had broken her fool neck in the fall.

"Get up," he ordered, not taking any chances with her.

"I can't," she moaned, "I think I broke my back."

When she whimpered and attempted but failed to get up, Longarm's anger turned to concern. He bent down to help her, but the wildcat jumped up and made a grab for his sidearm. Longarm knocked her hand away and pushed her face down into the dirt. He climbed onto her back, wiped his bloody nose, and hissed, "You have tried the limits of my considerable patience! I'm not giving you an inch of slack between here and Yuma."

Lucy struggled for a moment under his weight, and when it became apparent that she could not budge, she relaxed. "Get off of me, you big, bloody lummox."

Longarm climbed off. He drew his handkerchief from a back pocket and covered, then squeezed his nose.

"Dammit, I think you might have broken it," he snorted.

"You should have let me go," Lucy said. "I'll be nothing but trouble. I didn't kill my husband and I'll be damned if I'm going to rot in some territorial prison."

Longarm blew his nose free of blood. He had a canteen tied to his saddle and he used that to wash his face. "Let's go," he ordered. "We're taking that horse back to town and then we're on our way to Arizona."

"I wonder," she said, helping herself up into the saddle, "what terrible wrong you committed to be picked for this job."

Longarm mounted his horse and gathered the reins of the animal he'd commandeered. "I was told that this would be a plum of an assignment."

"You can't be serious!"

"I am," he insisted. "My boss, Marshal Billy Vail, painted a pretty rosy picture of you. He said you were young, beautiful, and a lady."

"Well, I'm sorry!"

"Don't be," Longarm said, deciding that his nose wasn't broken after all. "Two out of three isn't bad."

Lucy stared at him with his bulbous red nose, and then she actually smiled. "Even with a big red nose you are sort of good-looking. What's your name again?"

"Custis. Deputy Marshal Custis Long."

"Well, Custis. I'm an innocent woman."

"Sure."

"I am!" she protested. "But then, I'm certain that everyone claims to be innocent."

"Nearly," he admitted.

"Do you have any idea why we're going to Yuma by way of Prescott?"

Longarm scowled. "No."

19

"I've got enemies in Prescott who want to make sure that I never go to trial so that I can prove my innocence."

"You mean they want to kill you?"

"Exactly."

"I don't know about any of that. All I know for sure is that they say you shot and killed your husband."

"That's not true!"

"You can tell your story to the judge, lady. I'm just a poorly paid deputy marshal doing my job."

"Poorly paid I can believe. But you weren't selected as my escort because you are the boss's favorite."

"What is that supposed to mean?"

"Just that you'd better watch out," she said. "I'm giving you fair warning that I'll try to escape any way I can."

"You can't."

"And," she continued, ignoring him, "be aware that, if we actually reach the Arizona Territory, there are people who will stop at nothing to see me dead."

"Why?"

"Because," Lucy said, "my poor husband was a very rich man without any heirs except myself. And, if I'm judged guilty in a court of law, they'll strip away my inheritance. The ranch as well as all my husband's other assets will go to his thieving shirttail cousins and uncles. But I won't be judged guilty. And that's why they'll want to kill me."

Longarm looked sharply at her. "Are you trying to tell me that these 'shirttail cousins and uncles' murdered your husband in order to get his assets?"

"That's right."

"Any proof of that?"

20

"No," she said after a long silence. "After it happened, I was in shock and vulnerable. Instead of acting in my own behalf and trying to find proof that I was not guilty, I panicked and ran. I got all the way to Denver, and it was just bad luck that I was caught at the train station."

Longarm inhaled deeply and then exhaled slowly. "I tell you something, Lucy. I never met a prisoner that didn't try to play on my sympathy and then stick it to me the minute my back was turned. Now, I don't know if you are guilty as sin or innocent as the Virgin Mary, but I do know that I've got a job to do and that's all that matters."

"Is it?" she asked, eyebrows arching upward. "Can you just blindly carry out your instructions regardless of my guilt or innocence? Regardless of what is right and what is wrong?"

"That's not for me to decide."

She snorted with disgust and shook her mahogany mane of hair. "You seem like a more intelligent man than that," she said. "I'd hoped for better."

"Too bad," he said as he touched spurs and led them galloping back into Denver to return the horse he'd taken in order to catch her.

When they arrived in town, Billy Vail was in the street trying to calm the horse's owner, a tall, burly man who looked to be a freighter or a businessman of dubious background.

"There!" Billy said to the irate man. "I told you that my deputy would bring back your horse."

"You thievin' sonofabitch!" the big man cursed, grabbing the reins out of Longarm's hands. "I ought to drag your ugly ass offa that sorrel and beat your head in."

Longarm ground his teeth in silence. "I'm sorry, but my prisoner would have escaped if I hadn't taken your horse."

The big man stared at Lucy. "She's your prisoner?"

"That's right."

The man doubled up and guffawed so loud that he sounded like a braying mule. Longarm could feel his temperature rising to the boiling point, but he was determined to conduct himself in the honorable tradition of an officer of the law. If he could.

"Deputy, I'll take that pretty wench off your hands!" the big man roared.

Now Longarm had had enough. He started to dismount and shut the braying fool up, but Billy raised a hand to arrest his motion. "Custis," Billy said, "I'll handle this."

And as Longarm watched, Billy moved over to the big man and stomped down on his foot.

"Hey!" the man cried, hopping up and down. "That hurt, you little . . ."

Billy's fist blurred upward in a tight arc that ended in the big man's gut. It was a short, powerful uppercut, and Longarm could have sworn that it lifted the big man an inch off the ground. When the man bent over double and began to gasp for air, Billy hammered him to his knees.

"Thanks again for the use of your fine horse, sir," Billy said in a cheery voice. "It was an act of generosity and a real public service. Now, good day! And also to you, Custis, and especially to you, Miss Ortega."

Billy beamed and waddled back toward the federal building leaving all three of them to stare.

"I guess we might as well ride," Longarm said, taking Lucy's reins.

As they rode out of Denver a second time, Lucy clung to her saddlehorn. Longarm ignored the curious stares of the pedestrians, horsemen, and freighters that they passed and let the horses gallop until they began to get winded.

"How long will it take you to get me to Prescott?" she asked when they began to walk their horses.

"Maybe two weeks."

"Took me just seven days to reach the Denver train station," Lucy said with a superior smirk.

"Well," Longarm said, "you didn't have a prisoner to watch."

"That's true," Lucy said as she set her eyes on the Rocky Mountains looming up ahead.

Chapter 3

Longarm and Lucy rode south along the base of the Rocky Mountains. It was late in September and, high up in the deep canyons, Longarm could see that the aspen were starting to change colors. They were yellow mostly, but some were rust-colored, and Longarm knew that they would turn deep shades of red and ocher as the weather grew colder.

Lucy Ortega said little the first few days of riding. She seemed lost in her own dark reverie, and Longarm respected her wish for silence. He was content to his own thoughts, which focused on how he would spend his three weeks of vacation. He realized that there really wouldn't be enough time to float down the Mississippi River to New Orleans. So perhaps he would take a train over to Baltimore, Ohio, where he had a few friends. On the other hand, the weather might be turning to snow by then, and so it could be wiser to head south, rather than north. Longarm had always enjoyed Taos and Santa Fe, and he knew a few ladies who would be more than happy to help him pass the time.

"So," Lucy said one night as they camped in the mountains just west of Trinidad, "how long have you been a lawman?"

"About eight, maybe ten years," Longarm replied.

"You have a slight Southern accent," she said, watching him from across the fire. "Are you from the deep South?"

"West Virginia."

"Parents and family still alive?"

"You ask a lot of personal questions, don't you."

Lucy leaned back on her haunches. "I've been watching you, Custis, and I can tell that you are a very methodical man."

"How so?" he asked, turning a roasting sage hen on a stick over their fire.

"You move and talk slow, but you're pretty quick. I saw that much when you came after me on that horse you stole. You can be a hard man, can't you, Deputy?"

"I can," Longarm admitted. "This is hard country and the people I deal with aren't saints. You either have to play as rough as they want, or you don't last very long."

"Might makes right." Lucy smiled. "Is that your credo?"

"I don't know nothing about a credo, Miss Lucy. I'm just telling you the way things are."

"It sounds very grim. Can't you think of something better to do? Surely you've a few talents besides your ability to kill men and yank women from their horses."

Longarm bristled until he saw that she was taunting him. "I like what I do," he said. "I like the fact that

26

I'm usually outdoors and pretty much answer to no one except myself."

"Oh, really? And here I thought you were *ordered* to escort me to Arizona. Are you saying that in actuality you volunteered to do this?"

"No," Longarm grudgingly confessed, "I was ordered."

"Then you're really just another underling taking orders the same as any clerk or wage earner."

Longarm jammed the sage hen back into the flames. "You may think that," he said, anger in his voice, "but I look at it a whole lot differently."

"Why?"

"Because I'm out in the field and there's no one around to make decisions for me. When there is trouble, I have to make the decisions and they have to be right and made in a hurry. I don't ask permission from Denver to do this thing or that. I just act, and then I take responsibility. That's a lot different than being under someone's thumb."

She studied him across the fire. "I suppose it is," she said. "But won't you be promoted someday and wind up just like that chubby little man who called you his deputy in the street back in Denver?"

"You mean that fella that cut down the bigmouth with one punch to the gut?" Longarm asked. "Sure. But Billy Vail could leave his desk and come back out into the field. He'd just have to take a demotion."

"I'll bet he never will," Lucy said smugly. "Once a man gets a taste of power in the bureaucracy, he's forever addicted. Your Mr. Billy Vail is going to remained shackled to his desk until he slumps over dead."

Longarm figured the sage hen was cooked enough. He laid it down on a piece of leather and cut off the drumsticks. They were sizzling, and the juice was pouring out of them like the sweat off a fat man in the summertime.

"Here," he said.

Lucy took the drumstick, blew daintily on it, and then took a bite.

"How is it?" he asked, watching her.

"A little burned on the outside and raw on the inside," she said. "And it could use some salt and pepper and maybe—"

"Just eat," he growled. "I swear that you are a fussy lady. I guess that comes with having lived like a rich girl."

She tore off another hunk of flesh and chewed it thoughtfully for a moment before she said, "I was raised a poor girl, Mr. Long. About as poor as they come."

"I heard you were educated at some fancy Eastern college."

"That's true."

"Well, then?"

Lucy's eyebrows knit together. "I was raised in Santa Fe, New Mexico, the daughter of a poor but very respected doctor. We took chickens, food, sometimes a burro or an old milk cow as payment. My father was not only a doctor, but he was a humanitarian. He was too lax and forgiving and his patients often took advantage of him. My mother died in our two-room shack, and I doubt if Father even had enough money to buy the kinds of medicine that he knew she needed to ease her terrible suffering."

"Did she die of pneumonia?"

"A tumor." Lucy sighed. "She was a fine woman and her passing caused me great sorrow, but it actually broke my father's heart. He began to drink—a rather common malady in his profession. I think I would have watched

28

him die a drunken and a ruined man if the fates had not intervened in his behalf."

Longarm tore the hen apart and extended more flesh to Lucy, who stared into the flames and her past, lost to the world. Longarm waited for her to go on, but she did not.

"What fates intervened?" Longarm finally asked.

Lucy looked up suddenly. "Oh. Mr. Albert Buckingham. He was hunting in the mountains nearby with his son, a boy of about twelve. They were from England with a full party and were hoping to get a trophy elk or grizzly bear."

"But something went wrong?"

"Very. Mr. Buckingham shot a huge grizzly, but only wounded it. Those great beasts are extremely unpredictable, you know, and never more so than when wounded."

"They will usually attack," Longarm said. "Their attack is so sudden and ferocious that men have often lost their nerve and then their lives."

"So I've heard. But this particular wounded grizzly turned and ran. Mr. Buckingham, his guides, and their dogs dashed off into the woods after it. They trailed the grizzly for about two miles and the dogs were hot for the hunt. But then, a tragic thing happened. The grizzly circled around on them and went raging back toward their camp where the boy and his nanny were resting."

Longarm stopped chewing. He could visualize the situation. An enraged and badly wounded grizzly, circling back on its pursuers, probably to attack them from behind but instead chancing upon their unprotected camp to find a helpless woman and a boy.

"Are you sure that you want to hear the rest?" Lucy asked.

"Only if it has some kind of a connection to your Eastern education."

"It has *everything* to do with it," she said, continuing on with her story. "The grizzly attacked the camp and the nanny tried to protect the boy, but one swipe from the bear broke her neck. The boy ran."

"Not surprising, but the wrong thing to do."

"Yes, well, the bear overtook the boy and mauled him. The boy lost consciousness, and the bear had started to drag him off into the thickets when the dogs attacked. Three of the dogs were killed before Buckingham and his guides could arrive. They shot the bear and found the boy bleeding to death."

"And your father was able to save him," Longarm said, guessing the rest of the story.

"Exactly." Lucy wiped her eyes dry of tears. "When they brought the boy to my father, he was more dead than alive. But Father somehow sutured up all the wounds and managed to beat off the infection. It was almost a miracle that the boy lived and his father was so grateful, he offered my father anything he wished."

"Anything?"

"Yes." Lucy's chest swelled with pride. "My father wanted me to go to an Eastern school and maybe even become a doctor like himself."

"But you didn't."

"No," she confessed, "I was more interested in art and philosophy. And besides that, there was a tremendous amount of prejudice against women being anything more than nurses. So much so that almost all women doctors were educated in Europe. Did you know that?"

"No," Longarm admitted. "I've never even met a woman doctor."

"They are very common in England, France, and Germany."

"Is your father still alive?"

"No," she said, "he died about three years ago. Penniless, but beloved as always. When he passed on, I moved away. First to Albuquerque and then to Tucson."

"Which is where you met your late husband?"

"That's right. He owned a huge ranch outside of Tucson, but in the summer he and his family would travel up to Prescott, where it is cooler. They own several thousand acres of ranch land up in the pines."

"I see," Longarm said.

"We were married only a short while. Don Luis was a wonderful man. He was almost twenty years older than I, and had been married before but lost his wife. We were quite happy."

"But you fought," Longarm said. "There are witnesses who say that you fought on the night that your husband was killed."

"That's true. We were having a serious disagreement and it was our very first. But I would never have killed my husband."

"Can you prove that?"

Lucy's lovely face grew pinched and she slowly shook her head. "We were alone. I remember the scene very well. We were standing before a big rock fireplace and Don Luis was pacing back and forth. I'm not going to tell you what our argument was about because that is irrelevant."

"It won't be to a judge or a jury."

She took a deep breath. "Well, if I have to air the dirty laundry in order to save my neck, then I will. But suffice to say right now that we were both very upset. And then . . . then there was a single shot."

31

"Originating from where?"

"I have asked myself that same question a thousand times and I honestly don't know."

Lucy took a long, shuddering breath. She was clearly reliving the ordeal and shaken by the vividness of her memories.

"It could have come from a hallway but also from outside, because the windows were open and it was dark. I just don't know. All I remember is that my husband fell mortally wounded. He dropped to the couch and I screamed, then ran to him. I didn't hear them throw the gun that killed Don Luis at my feet. I swear it!"

Longarm wanted to believe the woman. It would have been hard not to believe her. She was pale and shaking, obviously gripped in the horrible memory of that moment. As he chewed on the half-raw sage hen, Longarm felt touched with pity.

"Then," he said, "you were framed."

"Of course I was!" Lucy cried. "The first thing I knew, three of my husband's worthless relatives came rushing into the house, and when they saw me, they began to yell. I was pulled to my feet and my gun was used as evidence against me."

Longarm stopped chewing. "Did you say *your* gun?"

"Yes," she admitted with obvious hesitation. "I had kept it hidden in our bedroom, underneath my nightgown. I hadn't seen or even thought of it for weeks. And then, there it was, the murder weapon."

Longarm resumed his chewing. From this little bit of information he could see that Lucy was certainly in a bad fix. He didn't know if she was telling the truth or not, but he did know that the evidence against her was substantial.

"So," he said, "you ran and made it look even more certain that you were guilty."

"What else could I do!" she exclaimed. "Mr. Buckingham's generosity had allowed me an education, but I had not studied law. I had no friends, and three lying relatives of Don Luis were pointing fingers at me. The wonder is that they didn't say they *saw* me pull the trigger."

"There were probably other people outside and they couldn't get away with that," Longarm told her. "At least, that's my best guess."

He frowned. "Was there anyone else in the house who might have shot him?"

"Only the maid and the house servants, and they were in the rear quarters, too far away to have done it. Besides, they all loved Don Luis."

"Or at least," Longarm said, "they pretended they loved him."

"What is that supposed to mean?" she demanded.

He tossed the drumstick into the fire. "It just means that *someone* killed your husband. If it wasn't you, and it wasn't the three relatives claiming to be witnesses, then it must have been someone already in the house, close enough to have thrown your gun on the couch or wherever it was found."

"Someone could have come in through the kitchen," Lucy said thoughtfully. "Perhaps someone employed in the stable or on the grounds. Someone who could sneak into our bedroom and find my gun, then use it and disappear."

"Of course," Longarm said.

"But how in the world can I find him!"

"I don't know," Longarm said, realizing that he had raised expectations where there probably should not be any.

"Would you help me?" she asked, her face suddenly lighting up with hope.

33

"I can't. My job is to escort you to Yuma."

"But you must have something to do in Prescott or we wouldn't be stopping there first! What is it that you are to do there?"

"I . . . I forgot to ask," Longarm sheepishly admitted. "I just plain forgot to ask."

"You're supposed to help me," Lucy said, nodding her head up and down. "I'll just bet that your Billy Vail or someone even above him ordered that stop in Prescott because the case against me looks fishy."

"Aw," Longarm said, "I doubt that."

"Will you at least keep an open mind about my innocence?" she pleaded. "Just take me to my husband's rancho and ask a few simple questions? If you do, you'll quickly see that I've been framed. That I couldn't possibly have shot my husband like they say I did."

"You're asking for a lot."

"I'm not asking," she cried, "I'm *begging!* I'm begging for my life."

Longarm reached for a cheroot and jammed it between his greasy lips, and then he began to chew rapidly.

Chapter 4

They had a hard climb over the Sangre de Cristo Mountains, and by the time they reached Albuquerque on the banks of the Rio Grande River, their horses were played out.

Longarm dismounted at a livery where he'd boarded his horse many times. "Get down," he ordered. "We'll put up here for the night and push on tomorrow."

"Our horses are exhausted," Lucy said. "I think you're either going to have to replace them, or rest them for a couple of days."

Longarm hated to admit it, but Lucy was right. They'd set a pretty hard pace coming down from Denver, and not only were their horses exhausted, they were in need of being reshod.

"Hello there!" the liveryman called, limping out to greet them. "Good to see you again, Longarm!"

Lucy glanced sideways at him. "Is that what you're

called in the field, Marshal?"

"Some people might call me that," Longarm said. "But my name is Custis. Or Deputy Long."

"I'd prefer to call you Longarm just like everyone else," Lucy said. "After all, by the time we reach Yuma, we're going to know each other very, very well."

"Maybe not so well," Longarm said, avoiding her eyes.

Lucy had been showing off a little these last few days, and she was starting to make him nervous. She wasn't doing anything real serious to unsettle Longarm's mind, but she'd begun sleeping closer to him at night and asking him to scratch her back and help her change her blouse. Things like that made it tough for a good lawman to keep from being distracted. There had been times when he'd even wished she was fat or ugly. That would have made the job far less taxing.

"Well, Longarm," the liveryman, whose name was Frank, said, "I've seen you with a lot of handcuffed prisoners, but I never saw one as pretty as this!"

"Thank you," Lucy said, smiling and batting her long eyelashes. "You are certainly a flatterer."

"Aw, shucks," the liveryman said, blushing deeply. "You're easily the prettiest thing I ever seen wearing handcuffs. What kind of a crime could a beautiful young woman like you have done?"

"She is accused of murdering her husband," Longarm stated quite bluntly. "And while the lady is definitely beautiful, I'm treating her just as I would any dangerous prisoner in transit. I need you to board and take care of our horses."

"For how long?" Frank asked. "They look right done in."

"They are," Longarm agreed.

36

"And I can see right now that they need new shoes. They're gonna throw 'em in the mountains if you don't let me tack on new ones."

"How much?"

Frank scratched his jaw. "For the two?"

"That's right."

"I could do both for . . . oh, twenty dollars."

"Fifteen," Longarm said. "That's the most they'd charge in Denver."

"Is that a fact?"

"It is."

"Then fifteen is good enough," Frank said, "even though we have to pay more for shoes and nails and such than them big boys up in Denver."

"I'll give you a dollar extra on the board bill if you grain both animals heavily."

"Now, that would be just fine!" Frank said. He looked at Lucy. "May I have the pleasure of helping you down, miss?"

"Of course," she said, shooting a disapproving glance at Longarm. "It's nice to know that chivalry still exists."

Longarm felt the insult and let it go. He dismounted, stiff from the long hours he'd spent in the saddle. He untied his saddlebags and bedroll, then removed his Winchester carbine and turned to Frank.

"Is the Buckboard Hotel still the best for the money in this town?"

"That it is," Frank said. "But I don't know if they're going to be too happy about your bringing in a female prisoner. Especially one so pretty."

"They're going to have to bend their rules and trust me," Longarm said, "because I'm not about to let Lucy out of my sight."

"She's slippery, is she?" Frank asked, eying Lucy with a bold and approving eye.

"She can be, yes," Longarm told the old liveryman. "She made a break for it in Denver and almost broke my nose in the process. I don't trust her anymore."

"Well for gawd sake don't shoot her if she makes another break for it," Frank pleaded. "Be a terrible waste of beauty. Be like stompin' on a pretty bird or butterfly or somethin'."

"Right," Longarm said. He took Lucy's arm firmly in hand. "Come along, Mrs. Ortega. We'll get a room and deposit our belongings, then we'll find something to eat."

"That would be nice," she said in a tart voice. "Your cooking leaves a lot to be desired. Everything is either scorched on the outside and raw on the inside, or else it's dripping in grease."

Frank chuckled. "Why didn't you let her cook, Longarm?"

"Maybe I will from now on."

"I'm sure that Marshal Putman would like you to put her up in his jail," Frank said, winking at Longarm.

"Yeah, I guess he probably would," Longarm agreed. "Maybe that is the simpler thing to do all the way around."

"Oh, no!" Lucy cried. "I'm not going to spend a couple of days rotting in some stinking jail cell while the marshal and his deputies leer at me."

"Marshal Putnam is a family man," Longarm said. "I think maybe that would be the better arrangement, providing you don't have to share a cell with more than one or two other prisoners."

Lucy took a step back and knotted her fists. "You just try and dump me in with a bunch of prisoners and I swear that I'll kill you before we get to Yuma."

"Like you did Don Luis?" he asked mildly.

Lucy couldn't throw a punch with her hands manacled together, but she did aim a wicked kick toward his crotch. Longarm was expecting that and he easily dodged the blow, grabbed Lucy around the waist, and gave her a rough shove toward the street.

"All right," he said, "we'll try the Buckboard Hotel. But if you give me the slightest bit of grief, I'll see that you're tossed in Putnam's jail until it's time for us to push on to Yuma."

"Why's she going to Yuma?" Frank asked, hurrying after them.

"Go back and take care of your business and let me take care of mine," Longarm ordered.

"But your business looks a whole lot more fun than mine!"

"Shoe our damned horses!" Longarm called over his shoulder as he marched Lucy to the hotel, avoiding the curious stares of everyone they passed.

"Marshal Long!" the proprietor of the Buckboard said in greeting as they entered the hotel. "What a pleasure to see you and your . . . what?"

Longarm watched the man's smile of greeting evaporate, and then slowly reappear under the warmth of Lucy's smile.

"This is my prisoner, Mrs. Lucy Ortega. We need . . . a room."

"One?" the man asked, eyes lifting in question.

"Yes, one," Longarm said. "I don't dare let her out of my sight."

"What did she do, cause someone man to walk into a wall and brain himself?"

"Don't be ridiculous, Marvin," Longarm snapped.

"Lucy is under arrest for a far more serious charge than that."

Marvin boldly measured Lucy until he felt Longarm's hot, disapproving eyes, and then he gathered his wits and said, "I have a room on the second floor. Room Twenty-eight. *Two* single beds. I hope that will be suitable."

"It will," Longarm said. "Give me the key."

Marvin gave him the key, and Longarm didn't even bother to thank him as he led Lucy up the stairs and found their room.

"Spartan," Lucy said when they moved inside, "but at least it's clean."

"And with two single beds," Longarm said, pitching his saddlebags and bedroll onto the bed nearest the window.

"I need a bath," Lucy said. "I feel like I'll never be clean again."

"I need one too," he said, "but even more, I need to get something to eat and drink."

"First," she insisted, "the bath."

Longarm thought that he probably ought to put his foot down hard and show her who was in charge here, but he was too tired to get into an argument, so he went back outside into the hallway and shouted down the stairs. "Hey, Marvin! We need a hot bath up here right now!"

"Two?" came the reply.

Longarm knew that two baths would cost him a full dollar. "No," he yelled, "one will do."

Longarm thought that he heard giggles from downstairs, but just when he had decided it was time to have a private word with the man, Marvin yelled, "One bath, coming right up, Deputy Longarm!"

"I'm going to need you to remove these handcuffs,"

Lucy said inside the room. "Otherwise, I can't get my blouse off."

When he hesitated, Lucy added, "Come on! I can't bathe in my clothes."

"Yeah, but . . ."

"You've seen a woman bathe before, haven't you?"

"Sure! But . . ."

"And you're an officer of the law, sworn to uphold federal law and not inflict yourself on prisoners in your custody, isn't that right?"

"Yeah, but . . ."

"And I *can* trust you to be honorable, can't I?" she asked as she begin to unbutton her blouse.

"Well sure you can, but . . ."

"Then let's not waste any more precious energy worrying about proprieties," she said abruptly. "We've been sleeping together now for several nights and nothing has happened."

"This is a little different, though," he muttered.

"Why?"

"'Cause I haven't had to be around you when you were taking a bath, dammit!"

"Aw," she said, dismissing his concerns, "just stretch out on the bed and close your eyes. Pretend that I'm your usual uncouth male prisoner. It'll be easy."

"I dunno."

"Sure it will be," she said with a toss of her hair. "Now please remove these handcuffs, because I sure can't bathe in my blouse."

Longarm could see no way out of doing what she suggested. He'd never escorted a male prisoner who'd been so insistent about having a bath. Normally, they just dunked their head in a horse trough or piled into a river and let their personal cleanliness go at that. But he could see that it was clearly going to be a different thing with Lucy Ortega.

"All right," he said, taking the key out of his pockets and then removing Lucy's handcuffs.

He was just about to warn her about not trying anything funny when there was a knock at the door and the call, "Bathwater!"

Not only did the bathwater come, but so did a big copper tub on wheels. All of this was delivered by three young leering men who could not keep their eyes off of Lucy.

"All right, all right!" Longarm snarled. "Just fill the damn tub and get out of here!"

"Have a good time," the last of the water bearers chortled on his way out.

Longarm slammed the door after them, and turned to see Lucy slipping out of her blouse. She wore a chemise, and before she could unfasten her skirt and remove it too, Longarm went over and stretched out on the bed. He removed his hat and placed it over his face.

"Lucy," he said after a few minutes, "I want you to have yourself a high old time. This might be the last private bath you'll enjoy for a good long while."

"Please don't say that, Longarm! I'm hoping that you will uncover my husband's *real* murderers when we get to Prescott and save me from ever having to enter that horrible territorial prison."

He lifted his hat and peeked over at her. The sight caused him to suck in his breath because Lucy had one leg in the steaming copper bathtub and one leg out. And what Longarm saw was damned near feminine perfection. It was enough to make him sigh wistfully.

"Is something wrong, Longarm?"

"There's a whole lot wrong," he said, dropping his hat back over his face and feeling his manhood stir.

"Well," she said in a throaty voice, "I'm sorry if the sight of my body offends you."

"The sight of your body, Mrs. Ortega, does a whole lot of things, but offending me isn't one of them, I can assure you."

Lucy giggled. "Men are so . . . so easily stimulated."

"You got that right."

"Just relax, Longarm. That's what I plan to do. I'm just going to lie here and soak for about an hour."

"I'm kind of hungry, and I wouldn't mind using a little of that bathwater too. Probably be cold by the time you soak, though."

"Oh, probably," she said without seeming to care.

Longarm closed his eyes and tried not to visualize the sight of Lucy Ortega's perfect white body poised over that shiny copper bathtub. It wasn't easy. He could hear the water splashing softly as she scrubbed the trail dust away and began to hum a song that he didn't recognize but liked.

"This is most pleasant, Longarm."

He yawned. "Glad you're happy."

"Oh, I am!"

"Good."

Longarm smiled. He wasn't going to let her get the best of him. Not hardly. He yawned even wider and felt the tension go out his body as he listened to her hum what he supposed might be an Irish lullaby.

Pretty song. Beautiful lady.

He wasn't sure how long he dozed, but it couldn't have been for more than a few minutes. All Longarm knew was that, when he woke up, Lucy was out of the bathtub and creeping across the floor, dripping water everywhere as she tiptoed forward intent on reaching his unattended six-gun.

When Lucy realized he was awake, she made a desperate grab for his Colt, but Longarm was able to clamp his hand over her hand and keep his gun in its holster.

"Oh, no, you don't!" he shouted, trying to sit up.

She was furious and on him like a wildcat, clawing at his face and trying to blind him so that she could either get away or get his gun. And when that failed, Lucy made a dash for his Winchester.

It was all that Longarm could do to jump up from the bed and tackle her as she tried to lever a shell into the rifle. They crashed upon the hardwood floor, Lucy as wet and wild as an alligator but a lot angrier and slipperier.

Longarm yanked the gun out of her hands and pinned her to the floor. The next thing he knew, Lucy was pulling him close and kissing his face.

"Stop it," he said weakly. "You're my prisoner, for crying out loud!"

"Shut up," she said, pushing his face down to her breasts. "What do I have to do, tell you right out that I've desired you from the moment we met?"

"Don't say that," he told her even as his lips found her hard nipples and she arched her back, bare wet legs lifting to cradle him. "This isn't supposed to happen. I could lose my job for doing this."

"But I *want* you to keep doing it," she said, throwing her head back and raking her heels up and down on the hardwood floor. "And a whole lot more, my darling."

If Longarm had one major weakness, it was for the flesh of a beautiful, willing woman. Lucy fired his blood, and when she blew in his ear and then put her tongue in it, he completely lost control. One minute Lucy was the only one that was bare-assed, and the next minute they

44

were both tearing his clothes off and he was mounting her.

"Oh, yes!" she cried, locking her legs around his waist as her body gave itself completely to his powerful thrusts. "Don't stop, Longarm. Take all of me!"

He did. He took Mrs. Lucy Ortega right there and then. She was so wet and excited and he was so energetic that they bumped and scooted most of the way across that wet, slick hardwood floor and they didn't stop until her head was up against the wall. By then, Lucy was squealing and bucking like a filly and Longarm was completely out of his mind. When he finally began to lose control, Lucy locked him into her body, and she almost fainted as her own haunches began to jerk convulsively.

"Holy hog fat," he panted when he finally caught his breath. "That was *really* something!"

"Yes, it was." Lucy stroked his back. "I hope I didn't rake you too badly. I just . . . well, Don Luis was never so strong and I completely lost touch with myself."

"Me too," he said, unknotting himself from her embrace and standing on shaky knees. "But I shouldn't have done that, Lucy."

"Nonsense," she said. "The amazing thing is that you resisted me for as long as you did."

"I suppose that's true," he said, feeling a little better. "You were sure tempting me, weren't you."

"All the time." Lucy stood up and her eyes went to the Winchester. "I promise that I didn't mean to shoot you. I wouldn't have done it."

He wanted to believe her. "Really?"

"Yes," she said, bouncing her head up and down and smiling at him sweetly. "All that I wanted to do was escape."

"And if you had, where would you have gone?"

"I don't know. I just . . . well, the thought of being locked up in the Yuma Territorial Prison completely unnerves me. All I want is to clear my name and try to start life over."

"If you clear your name, you'll probably inherit your husband's ranch."

"Probably, although his relatives are sure to contest."

"You were his wife. You'd have the best claim."

"I know," Lucy said, "but I don't think about that. Longarm, will you please help me?"

"I'll try," he said. "We'll stop in Prescott as I've been ordered, and I'll poke around and ask those witnesses some tough questions. Maybe I'll find a couple of inconsistencies in their stories. I don't know, but I'll try."

Lucy seemed to float across the room, and then she threw her arms around his neck, squeezed it tight, and said, "I am so lucky that you were the one chosen to escort me to Yuma. It could have been anyone."

"I guess," he said, feeling her hands slipping down his flanks to stroke his bare buttocks.

"Let's bathe together," she said, pulling away.

"You won't try to drown me, will you?" he teased.

"Of course not!"

Longarm climbed into the warm bathtub with Lucy and they arranged themselves real nice together. But while she splashed, hummed, and got him thoroughly aroused again, Longarm made damn sure he kept one eye on his six-gun.

Chapter 5

Early the next morning, Longarm was awakened by a
loud knock on his hotel room door. He pushed himself
erect, then reached to the bedpost and retrieved his six-
gun as Lucy stirred in her sleep and rolled over to stare
at him through one heavily lidded eye.

"Who is it!" Longarm called.

"It's Marshal Pat Putnam," came the reply. "I need to
talk to you right away."

Longarm sat up in bed. He had met the local marshal
on several occasions and had no strong opinions about
him, good or bad. Putnam seemed slow and lethargic,
but he was said to be honest and fair-minded with a
good grasp of the law.

"I'll meet you downstairs in about five minutes, Pat!"
Longarm called out. "Get me some coffee."

"Will do." A long pause. "Are you bringing the woman with you?"

"No," Longarm said, turning to look at Lucy, who was burrowing deeper under the covers.

"Okay," Putnam said. "But I got rounds to make, so don't keep me waiting all morning, Longarm."

"Five minutes," he repeated as he knuckled the sleep from his eyes and rolled out of bed.

"What does he want at this ridiculous hour?" Lucy asked. "For crying out loud, this was to be the first day for me to sleep in since my husband was murdered."

"Go back to sleep," Longarm told her. "I won't be gone long."

"You're going to leave me unattended?" She looked up at him with a question in her pretty eyes. "What if I try another escape?"

"I'll lock the door, and I doubt you'll want to risk climbing out this second-story window."

"You're right."

Longarm dressed quickly, and although he felt sure that Lucy would no longer try to escape, he buckled on his gun, collected his rifle, and locked their door on his way out.

Putnam was waiting in the small dining room, which contained six tables with red-and-white checked linen tablecloths. Longarm's cup of coffee sat steaming.

They shook hands and Longarm said, "I was going to come by and check in with you yesterday afternoon, but time just slipped away from me."

"From what I've heard about your prisoner, that doesn't surprise me," Putnam said with a wink.

Longarm drank his coffee and ordered breakfast. During the next hour, he and the marshal talked about one thing and the other, always coming back to Mrs. Ortega.

"So how come you were asked to deliver her to Yuma via Prescott?" Putnam asked. "The whole thing sounds a little strange to me."

"What is that supposed to mean?"

The local marshal buttered a piece of toast. He was a short, fastidious man who had once been a Pinkerton agent and who was reported to be very good with a gun despite his benign appearance.

"Well," Putnam said, "why reroute you up through Prescott if they don't have something ulterior in mind?"

"Like what?"

Putnam frowned. "My hunch is that this girl has probably convinced your boss that she has been framed. That being the case, he sends you to Prescott hoping that you can dig up some information that supports her story."

"If Billy Vail felt that way, he would have told me so outright," Longarm argued.

"Maybe he couldn't," Putnam said, munching on his toast. "Maybe he is sticking his neck out a little for this woman. It just . . . just doesn't sound quite right that you should be going to Prescott first. That's all I'm saying. I think that there is more to all this than meets the eye."

Longarm had to admit that Putnam could be right. During the rest of their breakfast, they talked about other things, and when they parted, Putnam picked up the breakfast check.

"It's on me, and I would like to meet this woman."

"Then follow me upstairs."

"Thanks," Putnam said with a grin as he paid the tab.

When they arrived back at the hotel room, Longarm unlocked the door and said under his breath, "She's a little tired and might still be in bed."

"Sure," Putnam said, grinning broadly as Longarm pushed the door open and stepped inside, not quite sure what to expect.

49

Lucy was dressed and was sitting on the edge of the bed brushing her hair to a luster. She looked, quite honestly, ravishing.

"Well, hello," she said with her sunniest smile.

Longarm introduced Marshal Putnam, who stared and stammered, grinning like crazy. "Pleased to meet you!" he finally managed to say. "I hope that you have an enjoyable rest in our town. Stop by to visit before you leave."

"Thank you," Lucy said, batting her eyelashes.

They made small talk for several minutes, and then Putnam said sheepishly, "Oh, I almost forgot the main reason for coming by, Custis."

"What's that?"

"The Kincade brothers were released from prison last month and they're back in town."

Longarm stiffened. After a botched stagecoach robbery attempt, he'd killed one brother and winged a second. The third had surrendered. It had been Longarm, not Putnam, who'd tracked them down, and the two survivors had sworn undying vengeance.

"You might," Putnam suggested, "want to leave town right now."

"Our horses are played out," Longarm said.

"Trade them in for fresh ones," the marshal suggested. "I'll try to keep an eye on those two, but I can't make any promises, and I can't just arrest them for what they've sworn to do to you."

"I know, Pat." Longarm's brows knitted together. "I'll go over to the livery and see how our horses are looking and if they're shod yet."

"They won't be if Frank is the one that's supposed to do it," the marshal predicted. "He's honest and he's a hell of a nice fella, but he's slower than a grunt."

"Thanks for the warning," Longarm said. "I'll see if I can build a fire under Frank's smokestack. In the meantime, you might just have a word with the Kincades."

"I thought of that, and decided it might be better to say nothing in the hopes that you'll be gone before they even know you were passing through."

"I doubt that will happen," Longarm said. "Albuquerque isn't *that* big."

"You're right," Putnam agreed. "There's not much that goes on that everyone doesn't hear about it. And I'm thinking that Mrs. Ortega has really got tongues wagging. Tell you what. I'll see if I can dig the Kincade brothers up. I'll create a little distraction to keep their minds on something besides nailing your hide to the livery barn door."

"Much obliged," Longarm said as they parted.

When Longarm arrived at the livery, Frank had their horses out and he was working on their feet. Their coats were brushed and their tails combed free of burrs and tangles.

"I can see you've been busy," Longarm said.

Frank dropped a hoof and straightened. He didn't look very happy this morning. "The Kincade brothers were through here this morning looking for you, Marshal."

"And what did you tell them?"

"I told 'em that you were just passing through and that the smart thing for them to do was to let bygones be bygones. But they didn't seem to cotton to that advice."

"How much longer until our horses are shod?"

Frank straightened, pressed his fingers to the small of his back, and groaned softly. "I don't shoe horses often enough anymore to be tough for it like I used to be. Besides, its a young man's work, too hard on the back for an old fart like me."

Longarm moved over to his horse and saw that all four of its feet were finished. Frank had just gotten started on Lucy's pretty strawberry roan. He'd pulled the shoes and was trimming up the feet and getting them ready for new shoes.

"Looks to me like you've got another hour's worth of work at least," Longarm said.

"No doubt," Frank agreed, nervously looking out through his barn door. "A lot of bad things can happen in an hour. Maybe you'd like to trade this little roan mare in on something else that is ready to travel right now."

Longarm considered this offer for all of about ten seconds, and then he shook his head. "Tell you what, Frank, the day that this poor United States deputy marshal has to sneak out of town to avoid a fight is the day that I'm going to hang up my spurs and six-gun and buy a rocking chair."

"Marshal, I ought to tell you that Jules Kincade has a double-barreled ten-gauge shotgun and he ain't walking around this town looking to shoot ducks."

"How is Lester armed?"

"Six-gun on his hip, probably a derringer up his sleeve."

Longarm checked his own six-gun. "After the brothers left here, which direction did they go?"

"Up the street," Frank said, pointing. "Probably have a few drinks for courage at the Delta Saloon, then come back down to your hotel. I'd not want to see either you or that pretty woman hurt."

"Thanks," Longarm said, heading off in the direction the Kincade brothers had gone. Longarm could see the Delta up ahead. It was a notorious saloon, known to be frequented by the worst kinds of men. The word that

Longarm had heard was that Marshal Putnam gave the Delta a wide berth because his predecessor had been shot to death there while trying to settle an argument between two drunks.

As Longarm marched down the street, he sensed that everyone along the boardwalk knew that there was about to be a showdown. Some merchants dashed inside and closed their doors; others fell in behind at a discreet distance, curious to see what would happen when the showdown took place.

Longarm ignored everyone and kept his eyes riveted to the doors of the saloon. He saw one man run inside, no doubt to sound the warning to the Kincade brothers that Marshal Custis Long was on his way.

As he walked along, the street became very quiet. Longarm had faced a lot of hard and dangerous men, and he had a feeling that the Kincade brothers would not try and ambush him, but would let their anger and hatred dictate their moves. Most likely, they'd come straight at him and hope to get close enough to give them a big advantage with the ten-gauge. Longarm knew that he stood little chance of surviving this confrontation if he allowed them to lure him into a shotgun's range.

Jules stepped outside, and froze on the boardwalk when he saw Longarm. He hesitated a moment, then stepped into the street and came sauntering toward Longarm. When he was about fifty yards distance away, Longarm planted his boots down solidly, shaded his gun butt, and yelled, "That's far enough!"

Jules kept walking and Longarm's eyes skirted the Delta, trying to catch a glimpse of Lester, who must have decided to try and get in a good potshot from a hiding place.

"Jules!" Longarm yelled. "I said halt!"

Jules finally came to a stop. He was a tall, stoop-shouldered, and slack-looking man who wore a leather vest over a filthy shirt. He had a potbelly, and his pants were torn and crusted with mud. His hat was a derby and he was chewing a cigar.

"Hello there, Marshal Long!" Jules called up the street. "I hear that you're passin' though town with a handsome woman. Thought it might be real interestin' to come pay her a visit and tell her what a hard-nosed sonofabitch you really are."

"I expect that she already knows," Longarm replied, his eyes roaming the dark shadows between buildings and then flicking up to the rooftops. "Where's your brother? The one whose shoulder I ruined?"

Jules's wicked smile went stale. "Yeah," he said, "Lester ain't never forgiven you for that, Marshal. I expect he wants to repay you in kind."

"Where is he?"

Jules shrugged, the shotgun swinging ever so slightly back and forth along his leg. Longarm knew that it would take less than one second for Jules to whip that shotgun up and unleash a load from both barrels.

"Where is he?" Longarm repeated, his voice taking on an edge of polished steel.

"I'm afraid that he's . . . well, he's with a woman. Maybe he's even humpin' that prisoner of yours right this very minute."

"And maybe," Longarm said, "you're about to enter a place called Hell!"

Jules choked a curse and swung the shotgun up so fast that Longarm didn't have time to do anything but react. His hand flashed down to his gun and it came up with the Colt bucking in his fist. Jules staggered with a bullet to the chest. Then he lifted to his toes like

54

a puppet pulled from above and the shotgun roared, sending a load into the earth about halfway between them. Longarm felt shot ricochet off the hardpan and cut through his pants. White-hot pain flashed across his eyes and he fired twice more, eyes locked on Jules, who took both bullets and sat down hard. Jules tipped the shotgun toward the sky, and as he died his fingers squeezed off the second load.

"Marshal, look out from above!" Frank screamed in a hoarse warning.

Longarm threw his head back and saw a flash of gunmetal in the sun. He dove headlong toward a wagon even as a pair of bullets stitched into the street where he'd been standing only an instant before.

Rolling under the wagon and out the other side, Longarm came to his feet in time to see Lester flying off the rooftop of a saddle shop and vanishing into shadow. Longarm went after the man.

Lester was on the run. Longarm could hear the pounding of his boots as he shot down a back alley, probably running for a horse that was hidden somewhere. Longarm sprinted into the dark shadows between the buildings and when he emerged in a back alley, he saw Lester tearing the reins free and struggling to vault onto the back of his horse. But he was in such a panic that he had spooked the animal and it was spinning crazily.

"Lester!"

The man fell off his horse, popped back to his feet, and threw himself headlong behind a rain barrel. "Come and get me, Marshal! Come and get me!"

"Throw out your gun or I'll kill you like I killed your brothers!"

Lester fired rapidly, but missed Longarm by ten feet. The man was badly rattled. Longarm moved forward, hammer cocked back and ready. "Lester, this is your last chance! Throw out that gun!"

"And go back to prison for trying to kill you? Fat damn chance, Marshal! If you want me, then you're going to have to come and get me!"

Longarm stopped and fired into the water barrel. If it was full, then his bullet might not penetrate both sides. But if it was empty, he was sure that his slug would find Lester.

The water barrel was empty. Longarm heard Lester cry out in pain even as he fired two more bullets into the barrel and sent splinters flying. A moment later, Lester rolled out from behind the barrel and went to his knees. He tried to raise his six-gun, but it seemed much too heavy.

Longarm stopped and watched as the man struggled with two bullets in his chest. Lester gagged and then he pitched forward, knocking the empty water barrel over. It had contained about two inches of rainwater, and now it leaked into the dirt, just like Lester was leaking.

Longarm reloaded his weapon, and he kept it clenched in his fist as he moved over to the dead man. He stared at Lester a moment, and then he walked over to the man's spooked horse and calmed it with a soothing voice.

"Easy now," he said, taking up the animal's reins and climbing into the saddle. "Easy."

Longarm rode back up the alley, avoiding the main street until he was behind the Buckboard Hotel. He dismounted, tied Lester's horse to the stairs, and hiked up to the second floor. He walked quietly down the hallway and knocked on the door.

"Lucy?"

There was no answer.

"Lucy!"

Still no answer. Longarm fumbled in his pocket for a key, and when he got the lock turned, he shoved in the door.

"Lucy!"

She yawned and raised her head. "No need to shout, darling. What do you want?"

Longarm closed the door with a deep sigh of relief. "I . . . I was thinking that I'd enjoy another bath."

Lucy pushed herself up on her elbows and brushed a tendril of hair from her eyes. "This morning?"

"Sure," he said. "Right now."

She smiled sleepily. "All right, Marshal. Call for the water, and I'll join you just as soon as I am fully awake."

"All right," he said, feeling the tension drain away as he locked their door and unbuckled his six-gun.

Chapter 6

Longarm and Lucy kept steadily moving westward for the next week. The country was littered with lava rocks for about seventy miles, and Longarm was very glad that he had had the shoes replaced on their horses. This was wild country, with a few isolated ranches and *rancherias,* most of which had, at one time or another, been pillaged by the Apache Indians who still ran free between here and the sanctuary of Northern Mexico.

"You were pretty lucky to have survived while crossing this country alone," Longarm said to Lucy one afternoon as they passed through a red rock canyon and struck out across an open, sage-choked plateau. "If the Indians had spotted you, it would have been all over."

"Just as it will be now if they spot us," Lucy reminded him. "But yes, I was fortunate. I saw very few men, and when I did, they were always at a distance. I'm sure they thought that I was another man."

"If they were far enough away, that could happen," Longarm said.

A few days later they rode through a petrified forest and admired the fascinating stone shapes made from ancient trees.

"Do you have any idea how this could have happened?" Longarm asked.

"As a matter of fact, I do," she told him. "I once read that this country was very heavily forested and then suddenly flooded with water. I guess the minerals in the water caused the wood to harden and fossilize. Anyway, that's the prevailing theory."

"My gosh," Longarm exclaimed with mock surprise, "they really *did* teach you something in that Eastern college."

She laughed. "I learned a great deal, including how to snare a rich Eastern husband."

"Then why didn't you?"

"I didn't like the East," she told him. "It was freezing in the winter and humid in the summer. And bugs . . . why, I never saw so many in my entire life!"

"Out here," Longarm said, "we've got poisonous scorpions, tarantula spiders, and rattlesnakes. They are far worse than any bugs."

"Maybe," she said grudgingly, "but there are plenty of poisonous snakes back East too. What I missed most about the West, though, was the vast panoramas. Back East, the forests are so thick that you can never see a distant horizon. I always felt hemmed in by those endless forests."

"I remember them," Longarm said, recalling his youth. "I remember the fireflies we had in the summer and the big warm rivers. My parents took me all the way across Virginia to the ocean when I was just a small boy. I recall the taste of salt upon my tongue and how warm the waters were. I told myself then that I'd live beside that ocean one day."

"But you didn't."

"No," he said, "and I've never really missed it. I've become a part of the West. It's in my blood and, like you, I admire the size and openness of it."

Longarm would have said more but, just then, he spotted a thin line of dust trailing off on the horizon. "Hold up," he said, reining in his horse and dismounting.

"What is it?" Lucy asked.

"Riders up ahead," Longarm said. "See their dust trail? It means that there are at least a half dozen or so."

Lucy dismounted, and her face reflected her sudden anxiety. "Apache?"

"I don't know," Longarm said, "but in this country you had better make that assumption."

"What are we going to do?"

Longarm scanned the horizon and saw a good place to take cover. "We'll walk our horses over to that big pile of boulders and hide there," he said, leading his horse quickly forward. "As long as they don't cross our tracks, they'll never know we were hereabouts."

Lucy followed Longarm, and since the pile of boulders was only about a quarter mile away, they had no trouble reaching it before they could be seen by the mounted horsemen.

"Hang onto my horse," Longarm ordered as he began to climb up into the rocks for a better view.

The rocks towered at least twenty feet over the rolling sage, and they afforded Longarm a fine panorama. He stretched out on the top of a boulder and shaded his eyes, watching the rooster tail of dust thicken as the body of horsemen drew nearer.

"What do you see!" Lucy called up to him.

"Just a minute. There!"

"There what?"

"Apache," Longarm said, pressing even closer to the boulder. "About twenty of them moving fast at an oblique angle to us."

"Will they cross our tracks?"

"I don't think so. Not unless they change direction."

"Thank God!" Lucy exclaimed, sitting down on a small rock and holding the horses. "I've heard horror stories about what the Apache do to their prisoners."

Longarm had actually seen the results of Apache torture. It was something that burned into a man's mind so that he would never forget.

"Are they raiding?" Lucy asked as she climbed up to join him.

Longarm turned on her. "Get back down and watch the horses!"

"But I tied them up!"

"And what if they caught the scent of those Indian ponies and took a notion to investigate? Can you imagine what kind of a mess we'd be in?"

Lucy, her feelings obviously stung by Longarm's sharp retort, hurried back down to the horses. Then minutes later, when the Apache were disappearing on the far horizon, Longarm climbed back down to join her.

"You didn't have to be so angry," Lucy said, pouting.

"Yes, I did. If these horses would have gotten loose, they might well have run into view of those Indians. And if that had happened . . . well, I don't think I need to tell you what kind of a fix we'd be in right now."

"No," Lucy said, "you don't."

Longarm loosened his cinch and checked to make sure both horses were tied securely. "It's getting late," he said. "We'll rest a couple of hours and travel by night. I got an uneasy feeling about those Indians."

"What does that mean?"

"It means that they were in a mighty big hurry. And when Indians hurry, that means they are either running from trouble they've caused, or going to raid. One or the other."

Lucy actually shivered despite the warm, high desert air. She untied her bedroll and spread it out on a rock, then lay down on it and said, "I'm going to take a nap. Wake me when it's time to go."

"Sure," he told her.

Longarm climbed back up on the top of the rocks and spent another hour watching the horizon. Just as the sun was starting to set and the sky was aflame, he saw another dust cloud and stiffened. Squinting into the dying sun, Longarm stared until his eyes watered and he was sure that the second body of riders were United States cavalrymen. He knew that because one of the riders had a brass bugle and it glinted like burnished copper in the dying sun.

Longarm jammed a cheroot into his mouth and chewed it thoughtfully for a few minutes before he climbed down to the woman and the horses.

"Wake up, Lucy. It's time to ride."

She had been sleeping so soundly that she started when he touched her arm.

"Easy," he said. "We've got to make tracks, Lucy. There's no water here and the horses are thirsty."

"All right," she said, yawning and coming to her feet.

Longarm tightened their cinches and helped Lucy onto her roan mare. The mare was clearly suffering for water, and Longarm's gelding wasn't doing a whole lot better.

"There's a little mining settlement about ten miles ahead," Longarm drawled. "It's called Rimrock and we can get food, water, and a room there for the night."

"I can hardly wait," Lucy said.

It was well past midnight when they finally dragged into Rimrock, and even the flattering glow of moonlight could not hide the devastation left by the marauding Apache.

"Hold up there!" an army private called, raising his weapon. "Who goes there!"

"U.S. deputy Marshal Custis Long out of Denver," Longarm responded to the shadowy figure guarding the pillaged town and the army camp.

"Your badge, sir?"

Longarm dismounted and dragged out his badge, saying, "Who's in charge here, Private?"

"Sergeant Wilder, sir!"

"Why don't you take Mrs. Ortega and me to the sergeant."

"Yes, sir!" But the private did not move. He was too busy staring at Lucy. "Who's she?"

"My prisoner."

"Your prisoner?"

"That's right. Now, why don't you lower your voice before we wake up everyone in camp and then take me to Sergeant Wilder."

"What happened here?" Lucy blurted out, her eyes fixed on the line of fresh grave mounds.

"The Apache hit 'em at daybreak," the soldier explained. "A boy of about fourteen, scared half out of his wits, managed to sneak off into the brush and reach our fort. He told us what happened. But by the time we got here, it was too late to help anybody. There

64

were seventeen killed. Six were women and—"

"Never mind the death count or the details," Longarm said abruptly. "Do you know who was leading the raid?"

"An Apache called Red Shirt. He's a bad one and we want him bad, but he raids and then escapes across the Mexican border where we can't follow."

"Did he take any women or children hostage?"

"We think so because a few of the younger ones are missing, according to the boy that escaped."

Lucy slid off her horse and had to hang onto her saddlehorn because she was so weary.

"Private, lead me to your sergeant," Longarm ordered.

"Yes, sir," the soldier said, coming to attention. He was obviously a green recruit and trying to do everything by the book. That would soon change.

Sergeant Wilder was snoring loudly when the private entered his tent. Longarm overheard their terse conversation.

"Sergeant, there's a United States deputy marshal outside and he wants to talk to you."

"A who?" a groggy voice replied.

"A deputy United States marshal."

"Yeah. Yeah. Tell him to go to sleep and come see me in the morning."

The private emerged from the tent. He shrugged and said, "The sergeant . . ."

"I heard him and his advice was sensible," Longarm said. He studied the army camp and guessed there were only five or six soldiers there. The others had obviously been pulled off to chase Red Shirt and his followers in the futile hope of rescuing white hostages.

Longarm led their horses over to a spring and watered them before he tied them to a picket line and removed the saddlebags and bedrolls.

"We've got some beans and sourdough bread," the private said. "If you're hungry."

"We are," Lucy said.

"Then follow me, miss!"

The private was more than happy to lead them over to the campfire, where a pot of congealed beans and bacon were pasted to the insides of a blacked iron pot.

"I know they don't look like much," the private said by way of an apology, "but they stick to your ribs and they'll stop your belly from growling."

"Thanks," Lucy said. "Are there any plates, or must we scoop the beans out with our fingers?"

"Oh! Sorry." The private jumped to a makeshift table and wasted no time in finding them plates and spoons. "Anything else I can do for you?"

"I don't suppose you've got a shot or two of whiskey that I can wash this down with," Longarm asked.

"No, sir! Captain Meeks won't allow no whiskey on patrol."

"Probably a good idea," Longarm said. He pointed off to the side. "We'll sleep over there and have a talk with your sergeant early tomorrow morning."

"Reveille is at five sharp," the private said.

"Great," Lucy replied. "That will give us about four hours of sleep."

"Sorry, miss. But that's the army way."

Lucy and Longarm nodded as they scraped beans and bacon out of the iron pot and began to shovel them into their mouths. They were famished.

"If you need anything else, you just holler," the private said. "I'll be on watch for another two hours."

"Thanks," Longarm said. "Do you have a feedbag and a little grain for our horses? They've been ridden long and hard."

"I guess I could rustle up some oats," the young private said, "but the army don't give anything away free. The sergeant will tell you how much they cost in the morning."

"Fine," Longarm said. "We'll be happy to pay whatever is fair. Wouldn't want to cheat the government out of a few cents worth of oats now, would we?"

"No, sir."

Longarm suppressed a smile and scooped up some more beans.

Chapter 7

Precisely at five o'clock the next morning reveille was sounded, and Longarm rolled out of his bedroll and swayed to his feet. The sun was just barely up, but there was enough light to see the devastation left by the Apache only twenty-four hours ago. The entire settlement had been put to the torch, and now lay in charred ruins.

"Good morning, sir."

Longarm didn't think it was such a good morning. The smell of fire and death lingered over the remains of Rimrock, and it made him want to leave as soon as possible.

"Morning, Private."

"I told the sergeant about you and your prisoner coming in late last night. He wants to see you in a few minutes."

"Fine," Longarm said. He glanced back over his shoulder. "But why don't we just let my prisoner sleep. It's been a hard trail."

"Yes, sir."

Longarm strapped on his six-gun and pulled on his boots, then went over to the spring and cupped a few handfuls of cold water into his face. After that, he headed for the campfire, where a coffeepot was already steaming.

"Marshal?"

Longarm turned to see a thickset sergeant waddling toward him. "You must be Sergeant Wilder."

They shook hands. Wilder said, "I guess this ought to convince you, Marshal, that it's not safe to travel this country alone or with a prisoner. Where are you heading?"

"Yuma."

The sergeant glanced over at Lucy, whose face was hidden under her bedroll. "The private, he says that your prisoner is extremely attractive."

"She is," Longarm said, "although I don't see what that has to do with anything. Pretty or ugly, they deserve the same treatment."

"Of course they do," the sergeant said with a wink and a smile. "Of course they do!"

The man's condescending attitude rankled Longarm, but he let it pass. "We'll be pushing on this morning for Prescott."

"Prescott? I thought you were bound for Yuma."

"I am," Longarm said, "but first I have to make a stop at Prescott."

"I see," the sergeant said, clearly not seeing at all. He glanced back at the Lucy's sleeping figure. "I don't think that I can allow you to go on without an escort."

"What?"

"Too dangerous," the sergeant explained. "My orders are to make sure that no civilians are endangered by the Apache."

"Don't worry about that," Longarm said. "We are going in exactly the opposite direction that Red Shirt and his warriors were heading."

"There are other hostiles raiding in this territory. I'll have to ask you to remain under our protection until my captain returns and can decide what to do with you. He may ask you to accompany him to the fort."

Longarm could see that this sergeant was too stubborn to listen to reason and was going to create big problems. "Look, Sergeant, I carry written orders—orders signed by a federal judge—to deliver Mrs. Ortega to the territorial prison at Yuma. Now, Sergeant, you don't have any orders that would countermand my orders, do you?"

"No, but . . ."

"Then I tell you what," Longarm interrupted. "Why don't we just enjoy a cup of coffee and then part friends."

"Marshal, I can't let you go," the sergeant repeated, sticking his chin out. "I got to hold you until the captain and his patrol returns."

"And how long might that be?"

"Probably a couple of days."

Longarm made a decision. "Could we step inside your tent and have a little private talk?"

"Sure, but it ain't going to change anything. You see, Marshal, it'd be my ass if I let you and that woman go and you ran into another Apache raiding party."

"I'll take the risk."

"I won't."

Longarm smiled and said, "Let's step inside for a moment and really consider this."

"Okay, but I ain't going to change my mind. You'll just have to wait here for the captain."

Longarm followed the man into his tent, pulled the flap, and then fisted his left hand and held it out to the side. "Do you know what I have in my hand, Sergeant Wilder?"

The sergeant stared at the closed fist. "No."

"Nothing," Longarm whispered as he measured his punch and sent his right hand crashing into the sergeant's jaw.

Wilder's knees buckled and his eyes rolled up in his head. Longarm caught him before he toppled over a table. He dragged Wilder over to a cot and stretched him out and covered him with an army-issue blanket. The sergeant looked as if he were sleeping like a baby.

"Give your captain my best," Longarm said as he rubbed his bruised knuckles and stepped outside.

Longarm moved casually over to their horses, which were unsaddled and tied to the picket line. He got them both saddled and bridled, then led them over to Lucy and prodded her into wakefulness with the toe of his boot.

"What, what?" she mumbled, groggy with sleep.

"Get up and make your bedroll quick. Tie it down and let's get out of here," Longarm said under his breath, aware that all the soldiers were staring curiously at them.

To her credit, Lucy did as she was told without explanation. Moments later, she was up and Longarm was helping her into the saddle.

"So long, boys!" Longarm called, waving at the staring soldiers. "Keep up the good work!"

They waved back and smiled, but they weren't watching him. They were staring at Lucy.

"Let's go," Longarm said, touching spurs to his horse's flanks.

They galloped out of what had once been Rimrock and headed due west toward Prescott, a town that Longarm had often visited and enjoyed. A town where Lucy Ortega had told him she hoped to find some answers that would keep her out of the Yuma prison.

They crossed the Painted Desert and climbed up into the Mogollon Mesa country, where the air was crisp and the nights were cold.

"In another few weeks," Longarm said as they camped one night high up near a stand of gnarled cedar, "there could well be snow up here."

"Brrr!" Lucy shivered. "I know that if I have to go to Yuma I'll wish it were cold, but for now, I'm freezing!"

Longarm made love to her every night, and they fell asleep wrapped together under the brillant canopy of stars. During the day, they were cautious and always on the lookout for Apache, but they didn't see any. Near Clear Creek, Longarm shot a four-point buck. He dressed the animal out and they feasted on venison for the next few days as they moved down off the Mogollon Rim country.

When they sighted Fort Verde, Longarm knew that they were almost to Prescott.

"Are we stopping?" Lucy asked.

"I'd prefer not to," Longarm said. "The army likes to try and run the show and I have my orders."

"Then let's just skirt the fort and keep going," Lucy said. "The sooner we get to Prescott, the sooner I'm hoping that you can help clear my name."

"I'll try, Lucy. But you have to understand that it might not happen. If you were framed, those people will have their stories down pat. They're not going to just fess up because I'm a federal officer."

"I know that," Lucy said. "But the marshal at Prescott was no help at all. At least you'll ask some hard questions and be trying to help me."

"Yeah," Longarm said, "I will do that much."

Lucy's eyes filled with tears. "I don't think I'm strong enough to survive a long prison term at Yuma. I've heard that it is a hellhole. That it's fiendishly hot in the summer and that the inmates live in dirt pits, like animals in caves."

"It's not all that bad," Longarm said, trying to reassure her.

"It isn't? Well, then what *is* it like?"

"It's . . . it's a prison," Longarm said, trying hard to think of something good to say about the Yuma prison. "It's situated on a bluff overlooking the Colorado River. In the summer, the guards escort the prisoners down to the river a couple of times a week to bathe in the river. I've seen them splashing and laughing in that water."

"Under the guns of prison guards?" Lucy challenged. "I don't think so."

"It's true. And yes, Yuma is probably the hardest prison in the territorial system, but it isn't hell on earth and the warden, whose name I've forgotten, is a fair and just man who treats the inmates well who behave themselves and follow the rules with respect."

"Longarm, please help me stay out of there."

"I will do everything I can." Longarm took a deep breath. "But Lucy," he added, "if I can't find any evidence that you were framed, I'm going to have to deliver you to that prison. It's my job and my duty. I won't turn my back on it."

"I understood that from the very beginning," she said quietly. "I knew from the start that you wouldn't just set me free. You're too much the lawman."

"Yeah," he admitted, pushing his weary horse on down the steep mountain trail. "I guess I am at that."

Chapter 8

As they approached the old mining town of Prescott, Longarm could see the former governors' mansion, and he was reminded that this town had once been the capital of the Arizona Territory. Surrounded by mountain ranges and pine forests, Prescott was high, cool, dry in the summer, and not nearly as cold as Denver in the winter.

It was a good place, Longarm had often thought, for a man to retire. There was a large, shady plaza in the center of the main shopping district surrounded by businesses and saloons. Ranching and logging had replaced mining as the number-one provider of jobs. People seemed content to live here and, to Longarm's way of thinking, Prescott had just enough activity so that a man enjoying his later years would not stagnate or become bored with life.

"Where is your husband's ranch?" Longarm asked.

"Just a few miles north of town," Lucy replied. "Do you want to go there first?"

"No," he said. "I need to check in with the town marshal. You said that he didn't impress you. What's wrong with the man?"

"He never liked my husband," Lucy replied. "They were not even on speaking terms."

"Any particular reason why?"

"In addition to Marshal Haggerty being abrasive and a bully, my husband always thought that he was corrupt. That he accepted money from saloons and such and protected them with his badge."

"That's pretty common, I'm afraid," Longarm said. "I've seen it happen time and time again no matter how good the man. Money becomes tempting even to a lawman, Lucy."

"Marshal Haggerty has money," she said. "More money than an honest small-town marshal can earn in a lifetime. I'm sure that he is being paid by the saloons in town to look the other way and to ignore complaints about cheating and prostitution."

"Well," Longarm said, "we'll just see how our meeting goes. These locals do not appreciate a federal officer coming to their town and asking too many questions. They have a tendency to get very defensive."

"Marshal Haggerty is going to be very upset with me," Lucy warned. "He'll want to arrest me, lock me up, and throw away the key."

"I suspect that's true," Longarm said, "but you're my prisoner now and my authority is greater than his."

"Don't tell him that. Haggerty is a very arrogant man. He'll listen to no one except those who financially support him."

"What else do you know about him?" Longarm asked, not liking what he'd heard so far.

"Not much. When Don Luis and I came to town, the marshal would be swaggering about and he'd glare at us. He never said anything directly, but I could see envy in his eyes."

"Envy?"

"That's right. Don Luis was a Spaniard and he was rich. He had a ranch and was friends with men in high places. That sort of thing drove Marshal Haggerty crazy. He knew that he could not intimidate my husband or browbeat him into handing over any money."

"I see."

"Only once do I remember seeing Marshal Haggerty approaching my husband. I was in a millinery shop and could not hear their conversation, but it was clearly unpleasant. Haggerty became loud and abusive, and I thought my husband was going to kill him or at least lash him with a quirt."

"But he didn't."

"No," Lucy said. "My husband was very self-controlled. He rarely lost his temper or showed impatience. I think that was one of the things that I most admired in him. It was so opposite my own personality and I wanted to develop those same qualities."

Longarm didn't quite manage to suppress a smile. "I doubt that you will ever be able to control your temper or impulses," he said, "and quite frankly, I hope you do not."

"Really?"

"That's right. You're fiery and impetuous, and those qualities make you all the more appealing."

"Well, I'll be," she said. "And I've always admire women who were cool and somewhat aloof. Who could be thrown headlong into any unpleasant situation and know exactly how to act."

"Those kind of women may seem admirable," Longarm assured her, "but they're often just incapable of showing emotions. And *that*, my dear woman, is certainly not one of your shortcomings."

"Thank you," she said as they entered the town.

Right away the people of Prescott stopped and stared. A woman like Lucy Ortega was not soon forgotten. The women who saw her fell into little clusters and whispered God only knows what, and the men stared, a few tipping their hats in respect and calling out, "Afternoon, Mrs. Ortega!" Or, "Welcome back, Mrs. Ortega!"

In each case, Lucy would smile and thank them for the greeting, but as they neared the marshal's office and a crowd began to gather, Longarm could tell that his prisoner was growing increasingly nervous about what would happen next.

"I wish we'd just gone out to the ranch," she whispered. "Longarm, I'm afraid!"

"Don't be," he tried to assure her. "I've got the extradition papers from our federal judge in Denver and my name is on them as the one who is to deliver you to Yuma. If Marshal Haggerty or any of his deputies . . . does he have deputies?"

"Yes!"

Longarm was about to ask how many when the door to the marshal's office swung open and a big bear of a man filled the doorway. Haggerty was as tall as Longarm and half again as wide. He wore a full beard, and the six-gun strapped to his big waist looked like a child's toy. Now, he glared at Lucy, then at Longarm.

"Afternoon, Marshal Haggerty," Longarm called, not quite ready to dismount until he tested the water. "I'm United States Deputy Marshal Custis Long and I'm escorting Mrs. Lucy Ortega to the Yuma Territorial Prison."

"Then what in the hell are you doin' here in my town!" the lawman boomed in a deep, guttural voice. "She's an escaped prisoner!"

"Being returned, as you can very well see."

Haggerty stepped out to the edge of the boardwalk. "Why, she ain't even wearin' no handcuffs or nothin'!"

"That's my decision," Longarm said, watching a deputy push out of the office and come to stand beside Haggerty. The deputy was the exact opposite of the town marshal. He was tall, cadaverous, and looked as if he were half asleep, except that his gun hand stayed very close to his Colt and his fingers were splayed, telling Longarm that the man was ready to shoot it out at an instant's notice.

"Mrs. Ortega, climb down offa that horse!" Haggerty bellowed. "I'm putting you behind bars."

"No, you're not," Longarm said, his voice hard and flat. "I have custody of this woman and I'm the one to decide where and how she is kept in custody."

"Let me see them damned orders you got," Haggerty challenged as he stepped forward.

"Can you read?" Longarm asked.

"Enough," Haggerty growled, sticking out a hand as big around as a pie with fingers as thick as sausages.

Longarm used his left hand to reach into his coat pocket where he had his orders. He slowly removed the paper and extended it to Haggerty, who snatched it from his grasp.

Longarm watched as Haggerty tried to read the judge's order. The man had fat, porcine lips and they moved when he read, halting every few words and struggling to sound them out.

"Why don't you let me read it?" Longarm offered.

Haggerty ignored him and kept trying to read the judge's order. Finally, he seemed to realize that he was making a fool out of himself in front of the townspeople. He stopped and a gave Longarm a twisted grin before he stepped forward as if to hand the order back to Longarm. Only instead, he pretended to accidentally drop it in a horse-watering trough.

"Oh, damn," Haggerty exclaimed with mock chagrin, "look at that, will you!"

Longarm could not believe his eyes. He jumped down from his horse, but the judge's custody order was already sinking into the trough, and when he snatched it out, the ink was running and the document was illegible.

Longarm was livid. "You did that on purpose!"

Haggerty stopped grinning. He drew his fist back and took a swing at Longarm, who easily ducked the punch and pounded the man to the gut, expecting Haggerty to fold like a wet dishrag. Only Haggerty didn't fold. His gut was as hard as rock, and when he roared, Longarm knew he was in big, big trouble.

Longarm retreated a few steps. "Marshal," he said, "this doesn't elevate our profession in the eyes of the citizens."

"To hell with that," Haggerty growled, charging forward.

Longarm knew that he could not stand up to the much heavier man and trade him punch for punch, so he hooked Haggerty in the brisket and took a grazing left to the side of his head in exchange.

"Get 'em, Haggerty!" a man shouted. "Knock his gawddamn head off!"

Haggerty had every intention of doing just that. Longarm circled, flicking out sharp left jabs to the bigger man's face, trying to blur his vision. Haggerty kept bulling in, trying to land a killing blow.

Longarm completely forgot the skinny deputy until the man tripped him from behind. Haggerty was on Longarm instantly. He hammered Longarm twice in the face and Longarm couldn't buck the man off. He'd have been a goner if Lucy hadn't spurred her little strawberry roan over the top of them both and knocked Haggerty aside.

Longarm came to his feet with his ears ringing and the taste of blood in his mouth. He had a mind to just draw his gun and shoot this big sonofabitch, but that would probably have delayed them in reaching Yuma, so he ducked a punch and whistled a right hand uppercut to Haggerty's exposed throat.

The town marshal blanched and staggered. He began to make terrible sucking and choking sounds interspersed with grunts as Longarm's fists pelted his brutish face. Longarm knocked Haggerty back until the man was pinned up against a hitching rail, and then he finished Haggerty off with a double-fisted slam to the base of his neck.

Haggerty folded, hooking one arm over the railing in an attempt to stay on his feet. Longarm grabbed the man by the ears and drove a knee into his battered face.

Haggerty was finished.

"Hold it right there!" the deputy shouted, gun in his fist. "One move and I'll kill you!"

Longarm looked at the man and knew that he was not bluffing. He was trying to gather his wits and catch his breath when a second voice, accompanied by the sound of a gun cocking, said, "Deputy Wilson, drop your weapon and raise your hands."

Longarm saw a tall, handsome man of about thirty step forward and disarm Haggerty's deputy. "Now, turn around and drag your boss back into the office and don't come out again until these people are gone."

"You'll pay for this, Brodie! Gawddamnit, you're making a big mistake!"

"Probably," Brodie said. "But you're not going to spill the blood of a United States deputy marshal."

"But what about the woman!"

Brodie looked up and smiled at Lucy, who smiled back, her face suddenly relaxing. She said, "Hal, I can't thank you enough."

"Sure you can," he said. "Clear your name and marry me."

Lucy's jaw dropped, and even Longarm looked astonished before he said, "I guess we need to talk."

Brodie nodded. "I guess so."

The crowd parted as Wilson dragged Marshal Haggerty off the street, over the boardwalk, and into the office. Longarm noticed that not one person even offered to help, which said a lot for Haggerty's popularity.

"It's all over," Longarm told the crowd. "Everyone go back to whatever it is you are supposed to be doing."

The crowd, however, showed no signs of dispersing. With Haggerty gone, they displayed something of a holiday mood, with lots of laughing and grinning.

Longarm felt woozy from the pounding he'd just taken. He went over to the horse trough, dipped his head in the cold water, and felt instantly clear-headed.

Brodie addressed Longarm. "I own a little cattle ranch just outside town. Don Luis and my father were close friends. My father worked for Don Luis for many years before the man sold him a little land on credit. I owe much to his memory."

"And," Longarm said, "you want to marry his widow."

Brodie blushed. "I didn't mean to say that. Really I did not. It just . . . well, it just came out." He looked up at Lucy. "I'm sorry if I embarrassed you in front of all these people."

"That's all right," she said. "Can we just get out of here?"

"Sure," Longarm said as he picked up his Stetson and used it to bat the dust off his clothes. He struggled back onto his horse and looked down at Brodie. "Lead the way."

Brodie nodded and went for his own horse. A moment later they were trotting out of town, and Longarm was left with a thousand questions about this man and his motives.

"You never said anything about *him,*" Longarm said under his breath when he thought that Brodie was far ahead enough not to overhear his words.

"You never asked," she said. "Besides, I always knew that Hal liked me, but I didn't realize he would ever want to actually *marry* me."

"Well, surprise, surprise," Longarm said drily. "Maybe he'll want to accompany us to the Yuma prison."

Longarm immediately regretted that caustic comment because he saw the pain it caused. "I'm sorry," he told her. "I didn't need to say that."

"No," she agreed, "you didn't."

After that, the three of them rode together in silence.

Chapter 9

Hal Brodie's ranch wasn't especially big by Arizona standards. Just a shade over ten thousand acres, but much of it was valley land and well suited for raising cattle. The house he lived in was a small well-built adobe and the barns were maintained, giving Longarm the impression that the operation, like the man himself, was very functional.

Little was said until they were inside the adobe. Hal motioned them to a seat as a maid appeared. "How about something to drink?" he asked his guests.

"A whiskey for me," Longarm said.

"Tea or lemonade would be nice," Lucy answered.

"I think I'll have a whiskey myself," Brodie said, easing down in a big horsehide chair and crossing his legs. After the maid left the room he looked from Longarm to Lucy and smiled. "Lucy, for a woman on the run, you look remarkably good."

"Thank you," she replied. "But given the circumstances, I don't see that we have a lot of reason for cheer."

"Maybe," Brodie said, "and maybe not."

"What," Longarm asked, "is that supposed to mean?"

Brodie's smile faded. "I was in Tucson buying some Mexican cattle on the night that Don Luis was shot and killed. By the time I returned, Lucy had been arrested and then escaped. I felt . . . helpless. Lucy, I knew that you could not have killed your husband, and yet I read the newspapers and saw the overwhelming evidence stacked up against you."

"Evidence in the nature of three witnesses who admit that they did not even see the shot fired!" Lucy said hotly.

"Exactly." Brodie steepled his fingertips and leaned forward. "The witnesses were Juan Ortega, your husband's brother and closest living blood relative, Manuel Padilla, a nephew, and Renaldo Lopez, a distant uncle."

"That's right," Lucy said.

"And guess who inherits all your husband's properties after his death?" Brodie asked.

"I suppose I will."

"Yes, but if you are killed, mentally incapacitated, or deemed morally incorrigible, then the properties would go to his brother, Juan Ortega."

Longarm blurted out, "Morally incorrigible?"

"That's right," Brodie said. "Defined in Arizona law as someone who has committed a serious felony—like murder."

Longarm took a deep breath. "Then we have a brother with a strong motive," he said. "But if Juan Ortega and the other two were outside when the shooting occurred, do we have a murder suspect?"

"I think we do," Brodie told him. "I was wrestling with this very same problem when I received a note. It is in Spanish, of course, but I will recite it in English. 'The *señora* did not shoot her husband. I know this and will tell you so for one hundred dollars.'"

"Let me see the note," Lucy said, "I can read Spanish."

Brodie went over to a desk, opened a book, and pulled out the note. He handed it to Lucy, who read it quickly and passed it over to Longarm, who had a fair knowledge of border Spanish.

Longarm looked up. "No signature?"

"No," Brodie admitted. "But I knew that whoever wrote that would come to me sooner or later. And she did."

"Who was it?" Lucy asked quickly.

"It was a young house servant, Maria Escobar. She came sneaking over to my ranch one night, very frightened. I brought her inside and, after she calmed down, I interviewed her. Maria said that she saw your cook, Miguel Rivera, fire the shot that killed your husband."

"Will she testify to that?" Longarm asked quickly.

"Not here in Prescott," Brodie said. "She's afraid for her life, and frankly I don't blame her. She says that she has seen Miguel talking to Marshal Haggerty and she knows they are all guilty of a conspiracy."

Longarm took a cheroot out of his shirt pocket, and this time he actually lit the thing. "We'll pack Maria off to Yuma where I know a good judge. When he hears her testimony and yours, I'm sure that I can make the arrests of those three relatives as well as Haggerty."

"Without proof?"

"You may have a point," Longarm said. "At the very least, we can get Lucy's name cleared and get Miguel

Rivera convicted of murder. As for the others, I don't know. If we make Rivera talk, we'll have a solid case."

"Is Maria still working at my husband's ranch?" Lucy asked.

"As far as I know," Brodie replied. "But the poor woman is scared half out of her mind. I was trying to figure out what to do when you and Deputy Long showed up today. It was clear that they did not want you poking around at your husband's ranch, digging up evidence that would blow this murder conspiracy wide open."

"Yes," Lucy said, "it makes a lot of sense now."

She turned to Longarm. "So what is our first move?"

"We get Maria out of Prescott and take her directly to the judge in Yuma. After she testifies, I come back and arrest Rivera for murder and see if I can get him to inform on his accomplices and avoid a hangman's noose."

Both Lucy and Brodie were nodding their heads. Brodie spoke first. "What can I do?"

"Nothing," Longarm said. "If you suddenly disappeared, it would sound the alarm."

"But he can't stay here without protection!" Lucy exclaimed. "Not after what he did to Marshal Haggerty's deputy today."

"I'll be fine," Brodie said. "I've got six good cowboys that all know how to use guns."

"Stay off the open ridges," Longarm advised. "Don't let yourself be ambushed by a sharpshooter."

"I'll be careful. That Deputy Wilson is a crack shot and has quite a reputation as a gunfighter. Haggerty, well, he's too lazy even to ride out this far. I don't worry about him. It's Wilson that I'm concerned about."

The maid brought their drinks, and when she was gone, Longarm said, "Now, Hal, tell me how we are going to steal Maria away from under the eyes of those murderers."

"I'll just offer her a better job," Brodie said.

"Just like that?" Lucy asked, eyebrows raising in a question mark.

"Yeah, just like that. I'm not worried about being shot by any of Don Luis's worthless relatives. Even his brother, who stands to inherit the ranch, hasn't the guts to pull a trigger."

"Maybe I should go with you," Longarm suggested.

"I'm afraid that would really put them on alert," Brodie reasoned. "It would be better if I went with a few of my men. I'll pretend that I am returning a stray horse or cow, then go inside and talk to Maria. She'll leave with me."

"All right," Longarm said. "But we'll be waiting close by, just in case there is trouble."

"Fine," Brodie said. "When would you like to do this?"

"How about first thing tomorrow morning?"

"Suits me," Brodie answered. "We'll leave after an early breakfast."

Brodie finished his drink and then gazed at Lucy. "I'm sure that you are exhausted. I have a guest room waiting for you."

"Thank you," Lucy said, looking sideways at Longarm with a question in her eyes.

"And Marshal, you can either sleep here on the couch, or in the bunkhouse. I'm afraid that I only have one spare bedroom in this small adobe. I apologize."

"None necessary," Longarm said, appreciating how neatly the Arizona rancher had managed to keep him from sleeping another night with Lucy.

"Good!" Brodie smiled. "If you two will excuse me

for a few minutes, I've got to go outside and tell my men what I want done this afternoon."

"Of course," Longarm said.

When they were alone, Lucy came over to sit beside him. She took his hands in her own and her eyes were dancing with joy. "Isn't this wonderful news! Can you imagine how happy this makes me?"

"I think so."

"Hal is wonderful to have done so much, and at such great personal risk!"

"He certainly has proved a savior," Longarm said, trying to dredge up enthusiasm. "Now, all we have to do is to get Maria out of your husband's house."

"She's young," Lucy said, "and I can well imagine that she must be terrified. I'm sure this has been a terrible ordeal for her, just as it has been for me."

"Yes," Longarm said.

"But it's almost over, isn't it?"

"If Maria will confirm what Hal just told us, I think that a judge will give me the full authority to arrest Rivera and clean up this mess."

"But what about those women prisoners that you were supposed to be in charge of transporting from Yuma to Denver?"

"Damn," Longarm muttered. "I'd entirely forgotten about them! Well, perhaps I can wire Billy Vail and he can send someone else out to bring them back to Colorado."

"I hope so," Lucy said. "It sure seems as if you'll have enough to do just arresting poor Don Luis's murderers."

"I agree," Longarm said. "The last thing I need on top of everything else is a bunch of crazy, cut-throat females."

Chapter 10

Longarm and Lucy sat quietly on horseback, hidden in a dense stand of cottonwood trees that were less than a quarter mile from the Ortega ranch house. Several minutes earlier, they had watched as Hal Brodie, accompanied by three of his cowboys, rode up to the ranch house. Brodie alone had gone inside to get Maria Escobar while his cowboys waited for the rancher.

"He's been in there at least fifteen minutes," Lucy fretted. "Do you think that anything bad has happened to him?"

"No," Longarm said. "And it's been more like five minutes."

Lucy expelled a deep breath. "What if they killed him?"

"Now why in the world," Longarm asked, "would they do something that stupid? They don't know that Maria Escobar is a witness to your husband's murder."

"We *hope* they don't know," Lucy said.

Longarm fussed with his horse's mane, trying to hide his own mounting nervousness. "Look!" he said, pointing. "There's Brodie and a Mexican maid."

"Yes, that is poor Maria. She must be scared out of her wits. And look at how upset Juan, Manuel, and Renaldo appear to be!"

Longarm could see for himself how upset the three Mexicans were at losing their maid. And although he could not overhear the heated conversation, he could see how Hal Brodie was practically throwing the Mexican girl on the spare horse that he had brought to carry her away.

"So far, so good," Longarm said. "It looks as if he is going to pull it off."

"He's acting very brave, isn't he," Lucy said.

"Yes," Longarm had to agree, "he is. Did you know that the man has been in love with you for a long time?"

"Sort of."

"Here they come," Longarm said. "We'll just ease back and keep these trees between us and your late husband's ranch house. Then we're on our way to Yuma."

"Poor Maria. I doubt she had any idea how much risk she would be taking."

"I disagree," Longarm said. "And besides, she has demanded a hundred dollars to come forth as a witness to murder. Don't worry about poor Maria. She appears to know exactly what she is doing."

Fifteen minutes later, Longarm and Lucy were galloping up to Hal Brodie, Maria, and his cowboys.

"I'm so proud of you, Hal!" Lucy said, eyes shining with gratitude.

Longarm studied Maria, who looked very frightened. "Do you speak English?"

"Yes," the small, pretty young woman said. "Not good, but okay."

"It's fine," Longarm said. "Do you know what this is all about?"

"*Sí.* I saw Miguel shoot Don Luis. And now, you wish me to tell this to a judge."

"Exactly," Longarm said. "But the judge is in Yuma."

Maria's face clouded with worry. "Why we have to go so far away, señor?"

"It's a long story, Maria. But the judge here might not be trustworthy. I can't take that chance. I do know the judge who presides at Yuma, and he's honest. You'll also be safer there."

"Okay. But first, the money."

Longarm started to tell Maria that he would have to wire for the money, but Hal must have seen his hesitation because he said, "I brought it in cash, Marshal."

"Fair enough," Longarm said, greatly relieved because he would have been flat broke if he'd paid Maria a hundred dollars. "Thanks. I'll make sure that you are repaid."

"Just getting Lucy's name cleared and seeing her husband's killers brought to justice is all the pay I need."

Longarm nodded and let Brodie pay the young Mexican house servant. She lowered her eyes as if ashamed to take the money, prompting Longarm to say, "Don't be ashamed about that money, señorita. I'm sure that you have a very good use for it."

"*Sí,*" she whispered, large, luminous eyes cast downward.

Longarm lifted his reins and gazed back at the ranch. "We could see that those relatives were pretty upset," he told Brodie.

"You damn right they were! Especially Don Luis's brother, Juan. For a few minutes inside, I thought he was going to go hunt up a gun and try to stop me."

Lucy's hand flew to her mouth. "I'd never forgive myself if you'd been killed, Hal."

"It's all right," he said. "Everything worked just fine. But I was thinking that I ought to come along with you to Yuma. You know, to make sure that they don't follow or anything."

"That won't be necessary," Longarm said. "In fact, it would be a dead giveaway to them that something was seriously wrong. We want those three to believe that you and Maria are back at your ranch and that everything, as far as you're concerned, is hunky-dory."

"All right," Brodie said, looking as if he had some misgivings, "but I sure don't like the idea of the three of you going on to Yuma alone."

"We'll be just fine," Longarm said. "Yuma is less than two hundred miles. We can ride down to Wickenburg, board our horses, and buy stage tickets. The line runs through Gila Bend and on into Yuma. We can be there three days from now. Probably take a day for Maria to give testimony, and then it's another three days back if everything goes without a hitch."

"A week," Brodie said, "and you can clean this mess up and it will all seem like just a nightmare come and gone."

Brodie turned to Lucy. "My dear woman, I don't know how you've stood up under all this. Losing your husband, escaping, and then being brought all they way back to Arizona expecting to be thrown in a hellhole of a prison."

"It will all pass," Lucy said. "Hal, it's going to be over soon."

98

Brodie reached out and covered Lucy's hand with his own. "*Adios,*" he whispered softly.

Longarm had seen and heard enough. "Let's go," he said. "We've got a long, hard road ahead. Maria, are you comfortable on a horse?"

She nodded her head.

Longarm pointed his horse to the southwest and set off at a high lope.

Maria followed close beside him, but Lucy lingered for a last word with Hal Brodie. That sort of irritated Longarm, but he knew that it was inevitable because, as much as he cared for the woman and as close as they'd become, neither of them had ever expected their relationship to last beyond this ordeal.

Wickenburg was only forty miles away, but it was a hard road and well past midnight when they arrived. The town had been born after a huge gold strike by Henry Wickenburg in 1863, when he'd opened his Vulture Mine. Almost immediately, the town had blossomed, within three years had become Arizona's third largest town, and had nearly been designated its territorial capital, losing by only two votes. It was said that gold fever was so rampant in Wickenburg's early boom years that the people had not even bothered to spend the time to build a proper jail for the prisoners that their lawmen arrested. Instead, they'd just chained them to a paloverde tree in the middle of town. The tree, still standing, was now called the "jail tree." Now, however, the mining boom was over and Wickenburg had settled into a quieter existence based as much on ranching as mining.

"We'll put our horses up and then find a room here for the night," Longarm said as they wearily guided their horses up the main street.

"Are we all staying in the same room?" Lucy asked.

Longarm had actually given that some thought. He didn't like the idea much, but he really didn't think he could chance letting either woman out of his sight. Maria might be having second thoughts about testifying and decide to run away, and Lucy—well, you never were quite sure exactly what she was thinking of doing next.

"Same room," he said. "I'll spread my bedroll out on the floor. You and Maria can either sleep together, or you can sleep on the floor too."

"All right," Lucy said. "Are you sure that there's a stagecoach leaving tomorrow?"

"Used to be one going out every morning. We'll find out from the liveryman."

They found a livery and awakened its proprietor, a rather seedy-looking fellow who was not all too happy about being awakened in the night until Longarm explained things to him.

"Sure, sure," he said with a yawn. "I'll keep your horses until you get back from Yuma. A dollar a day for all three."

"Fair enough."

"Five dollars in advance."

Longarm forked over the cash. "Is there a stage leaving for Yuma in the morning?"

"Bright and early," the man said. "Leaves just after sunup. Gets you to Yuma faster'n you could ride these played-out horses."

"Good," Longarm said. "What about a hotel?"

"Booked up solid. But you can sleep on my straw for another dollar. It's clean, and I'll wake you in time for the stage."

Longarm only needed to think about it for three seconds. They were all dog tired, and although he expected

100

he could find them a hotel room for rent, it just didn't seem worth the bother given the lateness of the hour.

"Good enough," he said.

The women were not pleased, but Maria didn't complain. Lucy, however, was not shy about expressing her displeasure. "For crying out loud, Longarm! I was hoping for a nice bed."

"You're so tired you'll fall asleep before your head hits the straw," Longarm told her. "We don't even have to walk up the street this way."

"Are you trying to save the government expense money or something?"

"Maybe a little," Longarm said. "As it is, I'm going to have to concoct a few extra expenses to cover the hundred dollars that I need to repay Brodie."

"All right," Lucy said with a yawn as she practically tumbled from her roan mare. "Which stall do you want Maria and me to sleep in?"

Longarm looked to the liveryman, who pointed do the line and said, "Third one down is empty and cleaned."

"Thanks a whole hell of a lot," Lucy snorted, taking Maria's hand.

Longarm shrugged, and the liveryman stuck out his hand for the extra dollar. Once paid, he began to unsaddle the horses and lead them out to a corral.

Longarm brought the bedrolls into the stall and spread them out on the clean straw. It occurred to him that he was probably sleeping with the two prettiest women in Wickenburg tonight but that nothing was going to happen. They were all just too dog tired and Yuma was still a long stagecoach ride away.

Chapter 11

Longarm awoke early the next morning when the sun was still low on the eastern horizon. Beside him Lucy and Maria slept peacefully, and although he hated to awaken them, Longarm knew that he must.

"All right, ladies," he said, "it's time to rise and shine."

Lucy groaned, but Maria started and sat up quickly, her eyes round with fright.

"Easy there," Longarm said. "Nothing is going to hurt you. You're safe and, in a couple of days, this will all be over and you can go onto something better in Yuma."

Maria nodded. "What is Yuma like?"

"Well, it's pretty hot there. A whole lot hotter than Prescott."

"It's hotter than hell," Lucy muttered. "It *is* hell."

Longarm ignored her and concentrated on Maria. "The good news is that you'll always be able to cool off even on the worst days by swimming in the Colorado River."

"Except that it is probably dry this time of year, although it regularly floods in the springtime."

"Lucy," Longarm said, "you're not helping things."

"Sorry."

"Maria," Longarm said, trying to raise the maid's obviously depressed spirits, "if you don't like Yuma, you can go on to California. There are some beautiful cities there."

She nodded, but did not look cheered.

"All right," Longarm said. "We've got to get moving. The last thing we need to do is to miss that stagecoach."

The two women were not very enthusiastic. But Longarm prodded them so hard that he was able to get them up and moving before the sun had fully lifted off the horizon.

"Where is this damned stagecoach line and why do they have to leave so early?" Lucy said snippishly.

"Because they want to beat the worst of the heat," Longarm explained. "The stage will hold over in Gila Bend for a few hours this evening, then proceed into Yuma overnight and arrive by mid-morning."

"Another night without sleep."

"Are you always so pleasant at this hour?" Longarm asked.

"I don't know because I've rarely been *awake* at this hour," she groused. "Are we going to have time for a cup of coffee or something to eat before we board the stage?"

"We'll find out when we get to the stage line."

"Good," Lucy said as they plodded along the almost empty street.

Longarm was thinking that it wasn't going to be a whole lot of fun traveling to Yuma with these women, but it was all part of his job. As bad as it might become, he never had any doubts that it was preferable to being chained to a desk.

As they were passing Howard's Mercantile, Longarm caught a sudden movement out of the corner of his eye and a well-developed inner sense told him that it marked danger. Without thinking, he threw himself into the two women even as two gunshots broke the early morning silence and a pistol flashed twice from across the street.

Maria cried out in pain and Longarm rolled, trying to shield them and at the same time drag his gun up and fire at their ambusher.

But the man was gone, probably into the alley across the street. "Maria, how badly are you hit?"

The Mexican maid had fainted. Longarm and Lucy both tore her blouse open and saw that a bullet had grazed her ribs.

"It's just a flesh wound," Longarm said with relief. "Lucy, take care of her while I try and get that sonofabitch!"

Longarm jumped up and raced across the street. The gunfire had roused the town and people were poking their heads out of hotel windows. A pair of drunks reeled out of an all-night saloon, and then reversed direction and almost tore the batwing doors off scrambling to get back inside.

Where had their ambusher gone? That was the question that filled Longarm's mind as he shot into a narrow corridor between two buildings and then pounded into an alley. He heard the sound of receding hoofbeats, and swore in helpless silence because there wasn't a horse on the street that he could use to chase after the ambusher.

"Damn!" Longarm swore. Who in the hell had tried to kill him? Had it just been someone out of his past, or had someone actually followed them all the way from Prescott?

Longarm had no idea. All he knew for certain was that the sonofabitch had missed and hit Maria, and now she would be so scared that she might even refuse to testify.

Longarm holstered his six-gun and hurried back to the main street. Maria was just starting to rouse.

"We need to find a doctor," Lucy told him, her voice strained and anxious. "The bullet might have broken her rib."

Longarm stood up and yelled, "Someone call a doctor! We got a woman that's been shot!"

Longarm crouched down beside Maria, who was beginning to twitch a little and come around. "Easy now," he said in his quietest voice.

"She's not a horse," Lucy said. "Just . . . just let me attend to her."

"Fine," Longarm said, "but we simply can't afford to miss that stagecoach to Yuma. We've got enemies here and that's why we have to get out of this town."

"But Maria has been shot."

"She's been *nicked*," Longarm corrected. "And if we stick around here another day for tomorrow's stage, whoever did this might decide to take another shot at me and maybe wound you or Maria."

"What makes you think that the man who fired was aiming for you?" Lucy asked.

The question brought Longarm up short. "You're right," he conceded. "It could have been any of your late husband's relatives or even Miguel Rivera, the man she says fired the fatal shot."

106

"Yes," Lucy said, "they'd want to kill Maria if they realized why we were taking her to Yuma."

"That's right," Longarm said, "but the shot might even have been meant for you."

"That thought has already occurred to me," Lucy said, her eyes tight with worry.

"And that," Longarm said, emphasizing his words, "is why we have to get on that stage. Once Maria has given her sworn statement before a judge that you are innocent and Miguel Rivera is your husband's real murderer, then we can afford to relax a little."

Lucy nodded with understanding. "I just wish the doctor would hurry up and get here."

"Here he comes now," Longarm said, stepping aside as a middle-aged man wearing pajamas and a robe but carrying his medical kit hurried up the street.

"How bad has she been hurt?"

"Not bad," Longarm said. "But you're the doctor. You tell us."

"I'm a *dentist* just filling in while the doctor is out of town." He leaned forward, peered myopically at the wound, and said, "Hell, you had me worried. This is just a scratch!"

"Well, for crying out loud!" Lucy exploded. "We're sorry to disappoint you."

The man scowled and opened his bag, which Longarm now saw contained mostly tooth-pulling instruments. There were, however, a few bandages in the kit. "We'll just wrap this up tight and stop the bleeding," the dentist said. "And I'll give her a little medicine for the pain. She'll be fine until Doc Hostettler returns."

"We're going to take the stagecoach to Yuma this morning," Longarm told the man as he began to bandage the wound.

"Well you can't do that, Marshal. This woman could even go into shock!"

"She'll recover just as well on a stagecoach as she would in a bed and she'll be in less danger."

The dentist wasn't pleased. "Hostettler won't be happy about this. But then again, he's in Yuma and you might want to look him up. He goes over there to do medical checks on the prisoners one a month."

Lucy paled a little but said nothing, and Longarm thought it wise to do the same. He leaned over to Lucy and said, "I need to get over to the stage office and purchase our tickets before they leave without us. I'll be right back."

"All right," Lucy said, "we're not going anywhere."

Longarm hurried down the street. He hated like hell to leave Lucy and Maria unprotected, but he really didn't expect that the man who had ambushed them would come back. By now, he was probably halfway back to Prescott.

Fifteen minutes later, Longarm had three tickets to Yuma in his pocket and he'd tipped the driver of the stage an extra dollar to pick up Lucy and Maria.

Maria was crying when they arrived and the stagecoach driver shouted down, "What in the devil is the matter with her, fer crissakes!"

"She's been shot, you idiot!" Lucy yelled. "So shut up and tend to your own business."

The driver shut up. Longarm grabbed Maria under the arms, and had considerable trouble getting her into the coach.

"It's real pitiful," the dentist said. "The poor woman ought to be resting in bed."

"If she stays here, she might be resting in a *grave,*" Longarm retorted in anger.

"You forgot to pay me."

Longarm pitched the man two dollars. He grabbed their bedrolls and his Winchester and shoved them into the coach with Maria, Lucy, and a heavyset middle-aged man with muttonchop whiskers and a stern bearing. Maria was still crying.

"I'm not pleased riding with a shot Mexican!" the man thundered as they collapsed on their seats inside the coach.

"Well that's too damn bad!" Lucy said, eyes blazing.

The heavyset man's mouth twisted into a sneer. "Can't you at least make her stop that infernal racket? She'll drive us all crazy."

"I tell you what," Longarm said through clenched teeth. "I have a suggestion."

"And that is?"

Longarm grabbed the man by his shirtfront, flung open the door, and threw the miserable fellow out. He landed heavily and yelped, "You broke my shoulder!"

"Good!" Longarm said, "because now maybe you'll begin to understand the meaning of sympathy. And besides, the doc is right here and waiting."

"He ain't no damn doctor, he's a dentist!"

Longarm slammed the door shut and dropped the curtain. The coach lurched forward.

"It's going to be all right," Longarm assured the women under his protection. "They'll be no more trouble."

They didn't believe him. Longarm could see that they did not by the expression on their pretty but frightened faces.

Chapter 12

Their stagecoach ride to Yuma was blessedly uneventful. Longarm had managed to calm Maria down, and although the poor girl was in considerable pain, he doubted if her ribs had been cracked or broken. True to Lucy's prediction, the Colorado River had dwindled in late fall to a mere stream and their driver had no trouble crossing the vast, sandy riverbed lined by willows and cottonwood trees.

"There's Yuma," Longarm said, trying to sound enthusiastic.

"And there's the prison," Lucy said in a grim voice. "I hope to God that I never have to enter its gates."

The prison was imposing, to say the least. It stood poised on a high cliff overlooking the river, and Longarm knew that its eighteen-foot-high adobe walls were eight feet thick at the base, tapering to five feet thick at the top. Walkways had been made on top of the walls so that prison guards could patrol around the perimeter twenty-four hours a day.

Standing defiantly overlooking the entire prison compound was the main guard tower, which bristled with a Lowell Battery Gun, which was an improvement over the old Gatling Gun. On a previous visit, Longarm had been told that the Lowell Gun was capable of firing more than a hundred rounds a minute into any section of the prison yard. In addition, at each of the towers there were armed guards with .44-40 Winchester rifles. To get in and out of the prison, you had to pass through massive, strap-iron grilled gates that swung beneath a thick archway that was heavily guarded.

"I think," Lucy whispered, "I'd just die if I had to become an inmate there."

"No, you wouldn't," Longarm said. "You'd find you had enough inner strength to survive."

"I don't know," Lucy said, shaking her head as they rolled up the western slope of the Yuma Crossing and into Yuma itself.

Longarm wasted no time getting Maria to the first doctor whose shingle he saw hanging from the front porch of his office, according to the sign a Dr. Clement Edwards. When the doctor had a chance to examine Maria's bullet wound, he was very upset.

"This girl shouldn't have been moved," Edwards said with disapproval as he rebandaged Maria's wound. "I can't believe that you would put her on that damned bumpy stagecoach. The poor girl must have been in severe pain, possibly even shock."

"We had her examined and cared for before we left," Longarm said, feeling guilty as hell. "Her life was in danger so we had to get here without delay."

"How are you feeling?" the doctor asked Maria.

"I will be good," Maria said.

"Well," Edwards groused, "they had no business putting you on that stage."

"How much do I owe you, Doc?" Longarm asked. "We've got to go find Judge Benton."

"He'll be at the courthouse," Edwards said. "And you owe me two dollars. I want to see this girl again tomorrow."

"Right," Longarm said.

He took Maria and Lucy's arm and they left to go see the judge.

"The doctor wasn't too pleased," Lucy said as they hobbled down the street.

"Well," Longarm said, "Dr. Edwards just didn't understand the way of things for us, and I sure never thought that I owed him an explanation."

The courthouse where Judge Harvey Benton presided was just a simple adobe that had once belonged to a wealthy Spaniard. It had a courtyard and eight bedrooms, the largest of which the judge had converted into his private study. The rancho's living room was now a courtroom, and while waiting to testify, visitors could enjoy a fountain and the courtyard's many flourishing plants.

"This way, Deputy Long," the bailiff said, leading Longarm, Maria, and Lucy down the cool corridor to the judge's study.

"Come in!" Benton barked.

When Longarm appeared, Benton stared, then removed his reading glasses and stared some more. He had once been a very large man, well over six feet tall and weighing three hundred pounds. Age, however, had put a stoop to his shoulders and he was beginning to lose weight. Longarm knew that the judge was in his mid-eighties and that he had been experiencing some health problems. It was sad to see that he was physically declining, although he still was able to perform his duties and then some.

Recognizing him at last, Benton said, "Deputy Long! What brings you to this tropical paradise again after such a long absence?"

Longarm ushered Maria and Lucy inside. "I have a matter of utmost importance," he said. "But first, I'd like to introduce these ladies."

After the introductions, the judge frowned as he looked at Maria. "You do not look well, señorita. Have a seat on my couch. Are you hurt?"

"*Sí,*" she whispered. "I have been shot."

Benton's eyes widened with alarm and they flicked to Longarm. "Has she seen a doctor?"

"Yes," he answered, "and she is going to be just fine."

"Who shot her?"

"I don't know," Longarm admitted. "The man got away."

"I see." Benton returned to his desk. He leaned back and said, "I assume this matter is of some urgency or you would not be here."

"That's right," Longarm said. "Let me explain."

When Longarm was finished relating all the details of Lucy Ortega's escape, arrest, and now her attempt to clear herself in the matter of her husband's murder, the judge leaned forward in his desk chair.

"Well, Mrs. Ortega, you have certainly had yourself quite an ordeal."

"I have," Lucy admitted. "And I don't know what I would have done if Deputy Long hadn't been willing to listen, then help. And if dear Maria had not also agreed to testify."

"Yes," the judge said, eyes turning to Maria. "And now, let me hear your testimony. Deputy Longarm, you will be the witness, and your own sworn testimony will most likely be required at some future date in my court."

"Or a deposition."

"Yes," the judge said. "That would probably suffice."

Benton turned his kindly gaze on Maria and handed her a bible to place her hand upon. "I must place you under oath to tell nothing but the truth, so help you God."

Maria stared at the bible. Her hand began to shake violently, and it was an effort for her to place it on the bible. Longarm was shocked by the inner struggle he was witnessing in Maria.

"Now, do you swear to speak the truth, the whole truth, and nothing but the truth, so help you God?" the judge asked softly.

Maria's lips formed a word, but it came out so softly that it could not be heard.

"Please," Judge Benton said, "you must speak up."

"*Sí!*"

"Very good," Benton said. "Now, calmly and completely, please start at the beginning and tell me exactly what you saw when Don Luis was shot."

Maria took a deep, calming breath. "I was in the bedroom when I heard the *señora* and Don Luis. They were angry."

"Having an argument?"

"*Sí.*" Maria retracted her hand from the bible.

"Go on," the judge instructed.

"I waited in the bedroom, but there was nothing left to do so I went into the hallway."

"And where," the judge asked, "were the *señora* and Don Luis when you saw them arguing?"

"In the big room." Maria's trembling intensified.

"But you could not see them?"

"Oh, yes, I could see them as I passed."

"And when," Judge Benton said, "exactly, did you see the cook—what was his name?"

"Miguel," Maria stammered. "Miguel Rivera."

"Yes." Benton chose his words carefully. "And did you actually see Señor Rivera shoot Don Luis?"

Maria tried to speak, but was unsuccessful.

"Please," the judge said. "You mustn't be so upset. There is no danger. I only seek to know the truth. Did you actually see Señor Rivera shoot Don Luis? And remember, Maria, you are under oath."

A loud gasp escaped from Maria's throat and she cried out as if in torment, then collapsed on the floor, weeping piteously.

Lucy dropped down to comfort her, but Longarm remained frozen in his seat, eyes locked with those of Judge Benton.

"Deputy, I'm afraid that there is more to this than meets the eye," he said.

"You think that she is lying." It wasn't a question because Longarm *knew* that Maria was lying.

"I'm sure of it," the judge said. "This young lady is very religious. She cannot, in good conscience, go through with whatever it is she is supposed to tell us. We need to find out the truth."

Longarm took a deep breath. Maybe, he thought, Lucy really was guilty of murdering her husband and she had put poor Maria up to lying for her.

"Maria," Longarm said, easing Lucy aside and pulling the girl back to her chair. "The judge and I do not think

116

that you are telling us the truth. You *must* tell us what you really saw."

It took several minutes for the Mexican maid to calm herself, but when she did, Maria seemed far more composed. She placed her hand firmly on the bible, looked directly into Longarm's and then the judge's eyes, and said, "I *will* tell you the truth. I will tell you who *really* killed Don Luis."

Lucy's hands went to her lips and she looked stunned as she took her seat again and stared at Maria before whispering, "Are you saying that Miguel Rivera did not really kill my husband that night?"

Maria nodded.

"Then who!"

Maria's chin lifted. She placed her hand squarely on top of the bible and said, "It was . . . it was Señor Brodie."

"No!" Lucy exclaimed, coming to her feet. "That . . . that cannot be!"

"It is true, señora. I *swear* on this holy bible that I tell the truth to you now."

Lucy collapsed back in her chair, her face mirroring disbelief. "But why would Hal kill my husband? And why would he claim that our cook did it? Maria, I don't understand any of this!"

Now that she had told the truth, Maria was composed. She looked to the judge, sensing that he was the one who most needed convincing. "I saw Señor Brodie kill Don Luis and then he saw me. I was so afraid. I was not even sure that my eyes had not betrayed me. Like the *señora*, I could not understand why."

"Because," Longarm said, "he loves Lucy and he wanted her *and* her husband's land. His intentions were to comfort Lucy, be her friend, and then win her heart

117

and hand in marriage, thus gaining everything. But he needed a scapegoat."

"*Sí,*" Maria said.

"And why," Longarm asked, "did he settle upon poor Miguel Rivera? Why not one of the relatives? Like the brother, the cousin, or the uncle?"

"They were all together outside," Maria said. "Only Miguel was alone."

"Is that all of it?" Longarm asked.

Maria shook her head.

"Then tell us the rest of it," Longarm ordered.

Maria sighed. "Señor Brodie knew that I hated Miguel Rivera. He had married my older sister and then left her with a child. So the *señor* used my hatred. And later, he came to me and said that if I swore that Miguel was the real murderer, I would not be hurt."

"Of course that would work to get Lucy freed," Longarm stated. "Because Juan, Manuel, and Renaldo all said that they only *heard* a shot. Remember, they did not actually say that they *saw* Lucy kill her husband."

"Yes," Lucy exclaimed, "that's right!"

Longarm came to his feet. "It all figured to work out perfect for Hal Brodie. He wanted Lucy, and in Miguel he found his scapegoat. Later, he helped Lucy escape without her even knowing it, and then he even coerced poor Maria into coming here and testifying that she actually saw the cook, Miguel Rivera, kill Don Luis."

Judge Benton leaned back in his chair and smiled. "Maria, has the deputy explained everything correctly?"

"*Sí,*" Maria said. "I did not want to lie! But Señor Brodie said that I would be killed if I did not and that it was only justice that Miguel would be sent to prison."

"And you would be paid in addition to the hundred dollars you asked from me?" Longarm said.

"*Sí,*" Maria said, nodding her head up and down. "Señor Brodie promised to pay me five hundred dollars, but I was never to return to Prescott."

"And that's it?" the judge asked.

"As God is my witness, I have told you everything," Maria said, eyes filling with tears. "And now, Judge, will you send *me* to prison?"

"Of course not." Benton beamed. "My dear girl, none of this was your doing! What else could you do but agree to lie saying that Miguel killed Don Luis? To have refused would have been your own death sentence."

Maria managed a smile. "I cannot go back to Prescott. I must go away."

"Don't worry about Hal Brodie," Longarm said. "I'll see that he is arrested and brought to justice for the murder of Don Luis."

Judge Benton came to his feet. "This has been a most interesting session. Maria, Miss Ortega, I must insist that you remain in Yuma until this matter is cleared up. It should not take more time than is necessary for Deputy Long to arrest and escort Mr. Brodie to the Yuma Territorial Prison for trial."

They nodded.

The judge looked to Longarm and said, "How soon can you return to Prescott and arrest Brodie?"

"I can leave on the first stage."

"Good! Then do so."

There wasn't much left to say after that. Longarm excused himself and the others, then went to find Lucy and Maria suitable lodging while he returned to Prescott and made his arrest.

"I can't believe that I'm free of this," Lucy said the next afternoon as Longarm prepared to board the stage back to Prescott. "It seems unreal that Hal Brodie is my husband's killer. He was so nice."

"Too damn nice," Longarm said. "There was just something wrong about that man from the first moment we met. At first, I attributed it to petty jealousy."

"You were jealous of Hal?" Lucy asked.

"Yes," Longarm admitted. "But I also sensed he was lying about something. I never suspected that he was actually Don Luis's killer."

"Be careful," Lucy said, kissing Longarm good-bye.

"Don't worry," Longarm promised as he climbed on board the stage, "I will."

Longarm was off then, riding across the stream that was now the Colorado River and returning to Prescott. In another week, he hoped, this case would all be over and he could telegraph Billy Vail and tell him the entire remarkable story.

Chapter 13

Longarm was jarred to jelly by the time he finally got back to Wickenburg. He'd spent most of a week sitting in a miserable stagecoach that traveled across the most boring and inhospitable land in all of North America. He was exhausted, out of sorts, and in serious need of sleep and rest. Even his legs felt rubbery when he finally came to rest on solid ground.

"Honey," a melodious voice said, "you look like you been dragged through a knothole ass backward."

Longarm pulled his Winchester and saddlebags from the coach and turned to see who had spoken to him. He blinked and then smiled. "Betsy?"

She was big and exceedingly buxom, with long blond hair and cute double chins that wagged when she nodded her head. With a squeal of delight, Betsy grabbed Longarm and locked him in a crushing embrace, mashing his lips into his teeth.

"Honey," she yelled, loud enough for half of Wickenburg to hear, "I just arrived from Santa Fe and was planning to go on over to San Diego tomorrow or the next day!"

Longarm struggled free. "Why, Betsy, you have *grown!*"

She giggled and pranced with the lightness of a draft horse. "I have put on a few extra pounds," she admitted, "but you always said you liked your women big and strong."

Longarm didn't recall saying that. Betsy York, when last he'd seen her some five years before in a place he couldn't exactly remember, had been about a hundred pounds lighter. But she still wore the same overpowering perfume and had that same raucous laugh that started at the belly and floated through her nostrils to make them quiver like bowstrings.

"Well," Longarm said. "It's been quite a while, all right. How have you been?"

"Missin' a man like you, honey-pie! Where are we staying tonight?"

Longarm gulped. "Well, listen, Betsy," he said, not wishing to hurt her feelings but definitely not up to spending the night in bed with this behemoth. "I . . . I'm just all dogged out and I was planning to get a good night's sleep and . . ."

"Aw, we can sleep in the grave!" she howled, slipping her thick, bracelet-ringed arm around his waist and dragging him up to his toes. "I got a nice room in the Baltimore Hotel and a great big bed that we can fill up together."

"Shhh!" Longarm said, noticing how everyone was staring. "Really, Betsy, I need some rest."

"Then you shall have it! Come on up to my room, stretch out, and let me call the hotel desk for a bath and some champagne. Honey, have you got any money?"

"Some, but . . ."

"Good!"

"But what about your trip to San Diego?"

"Oh, hell," Betsy said, waving off the thought, "this stagecoach leaves bright and early every morning. I can go there any old time, but I sure can't wait to get re-acquainted with an old lover-boy like you."

Had he not been so tired and his defenses at an all-time low, Longarm would have broken free and insisted that he get his own room. Then he would have somehow managed to avoid Betsy York until she tired of waiting for him while he found and arrested Hal Brodie.

"Listen, Betsy, I . . ."

"Here," she said, "I'll carry that rifle and those saddlebags. You just look plumb tuckered out."

"I am about to fall asleep on my feet, Betsy."

"Well, then, let's get you to bed. Want a meal and a bath first?"

"I could use both."

"Give me some money and I'll order us a couple of chickens brought up from this wonderful restaurant that I ever saw. It smelled so good I was droolin' as I passed. They got a sign in the window saying you can buy a whole fried chicken for one dollar. I expect we could each eat one or two."

"Yeah," Longarm said weakly as she led him away from the stagecoach office.

Twenty minutes later, Longarm was soaking in a bathtub devouring a couple of chicken wings and drumsticks while Betsy did the major damage on the three chickens that had been sent up to their room.

"Well, honey, you've gotten a little skinnier and I've gotten a little fatter since we last were together," Betsy said, wiping the grease from her lips with the back of her arm. "But I'll bet that we're still a pair of frisky lovers."

"Betsy, I told you that I was just wrung out. I doubt that I could be any fun at all tonight."

"Well, we'll just see about that!" she said, giggling.

Longarm finished his bath, and washed the chicken down with champagne that Betsy had ordered to mark this occasion.

"Here," she said, bringing him a towel when he was all done. "Just climb out of that tub and let Mama pat you dry."

"I can dry myself," he said, stifling a yawn.

"Of course you can! But you'll like it better when I do it for you."

Longarm stood up in the tub and let Betsy dry his hair and then work down across his chest. She was grinning and thoroughly enjoying herself, moving around him like she was polishing a bronze statue. He had to admit that, as she rubbed his body briskly with the towel, he did feel revived. In fact he revived too much, because Betsy howled and pointed at his thickening manhood.

"Would you look at that young man stand at attention and give Mama a salute!"

Longarm glanced down and saw that he was betrayed by an erection. "It's just that you've been rubbing it," he said lamely. "It doesn't mean anything."

"Of course it does!"

Betsy dropped down to her knees hard enough to cause the floor to shake and the surface of the water to ripple. She took the "young man" in her mouth and gripped Longarm's buttocks with her greasy fingers.

"Ummm-ummm!" she murmured. "You're my dessert, honey!"

Longarm just stood there up to his knees in warm bathwater, thinking he ought to protest but finding he hadn't the willpower. So he wiped his own greasy hands on his chest, patted Betsy's head, and closed his eyes with a sigh of contentment.

"Honey," she said ten minutes later, "your skinny little legs are startin' to bow like a pair of wishbones. Let's get you over to the bed and get down to business."

Longarm had decided that it was impossible to resist Betsy any longer, so he slopped out of the tub, padded wetly over to the bed, and collapsed. Betsy peeled off her clothes, and she was even bigger than Longarm had imagined. Three hundred pounds if she weighed an ounce. Longarm was wondering how he was going to handle this when she hopped onto him, causing the bed to groan and nearly buckle.

"Uggg!" Longarm grunted as her thick, powerful thighs clamped onto his waist and she slapped her immense bottom down hard on his stiff rod.

"Feels like old times, don't it!" she gushed. "Maybe you've shrunk a little, but not so's I can't enjoy you."

"I think," Longarm gasped, "you've just grown a little bigger."

That caused Betsy to howl with mirth. But soon she was squashing Longarm down into the mattress and grunting like a pen of pigs as she worked over him. To his surprise, Longarm found that he was still able to breathe and that Betsy, while she might have ballooned to gargantuan proportions, still knew how to drive a man to the heights of ecstasy.

"Oh, honey," she moaned, "we're gonna have a *wonderful* time! All night long!"

Longarm tried to suck in enough breath to mount a protest, but couldn't. With all his strength, he managed to roll Betsy over onto her back and she loved it.

"I never forgot you," Betsy said, her chins jiggling as he began to plunge in and out of her. "Never forgot how good you did it to me that night in Abilene."

"Was that where it was?"

"Oh, yes, honey! I was just seventeen and you were the first man who really taught me how good it could be."

"I'm glad," Longarm panted, "that I could do that for you, Betsy."

"Whooo-wee!" she squealed as her body exploded like an erupting volcano.

Longarm rode Betsy to the finish line, and then he rolled off and collapsed into a state of near-unconsciousness.

Longarm awakened to find her snoring but wearing a broad smile early the next morning. He couldn't exactly remember how many times Betsy had awakened him in the night to satisfy her great, hungry body, but it had to have been three or four times at least.

The amazing thing was that Longarm felt good. Kinda loose in the guts, but good. His hands were steady and his mind was clear, probably because she'd drunk almost all of the champagne. In a fit of guilt for leaving Betsy, Longarm left ten dollars on her bedside—enough, he hoped, to buy her that stagecoach ride to San Diego.

"Good-bye, Betsy," Longarm said as he stood by the door. "It was worth a memory."

As if she heard him, Betsy snorted, lips fluttering as she rolled over and crushed a pillow to her mammoth breasts.

Chapter 14

Longarm headed for the livery in order to reclaim his horse. The proprietor was mucking out stalls when Longarm appeared.

"Hello there!" Longarm called.

The liveryman turned and leaned on his pitchfork. "Well, I'll be damned! It's the marshal. Say, where are those two pretty women you had with you the last time through?"

"They're in Yuma."

"Hell of a place to leave 'em."

"I guess," Longarm said. "I'm here to claim my horse."

"He's waitin' along with the other two horses. You owe me a little board bill, though."

"I figured I did," Longarm said, digging into his pants for some cash. When they settled up, Longarm dusted off his saddle and led his gelding out of its stall. "He looks a whole lot more rested."

"He is," the man said. "You gonna come back and get the other horses?"

"I expect I will in a day or two," Longarm said, thinking that it would take that long to arrest Hal Brodie and bring him back down from Prescott.

"What then?"

"I'm not altogether sure," Longarm said, not wishing to discuss his plans with anyone.

"You gonna bring them pretty women back?"

"Maybe."

"I hope you do," the liveryman said with a lascivious grin. "I told everyone about you and them all sleepin' together in my stall. I bet you had a real high old time with them pretty fillies."

Longarm's voice turned rough. "You talk too damn much, know that?"

The liveryman's eyes widened and he tried to bluster. "Well, I didn't know what you was doin' was a secret!"

Longarm saddled his gelding and tied his bedroll down tight behind the cantle. Without a word, he mounted his horse and rode out of Wickenburg. It was midday and the next forty miles were all uphill to Prescott.

He arrived back at Prescott around midnight and found a corral for his horse at the livery, then went to a cheap hotel and fell asleep the minute his head hit the mattress. Early the next morning Longarm made it a point to avoid being seen by Marshal Haggerty. All he wanted to do was to ride out to the Brodie Ranch, arrest Hal for murder, and get them both back down to Wickenburg. At that point, they could board the stagecoach that would carry them safely to Yuma. After that, he could think about returning to Colorado, which to Longarm's way of thinking couldn't possibly happen fast enough.

Half starved, Longarm found a little cafe that served a mighty fine breakfast of biscuits and gravy, eggs, a tough but sizable steak, and all the coffee your gut could stand for only six bits. Longarm hadn't realized how famished he'd been, and Betsy had been right, he was a little hollow in the gut and starved-looking.

"Aren't you that Marshal Long?" a cute little waitress asked with a smile that warmed him as much as the coffee.

"I am," Longarm said, "but I'd just as soon not spread the news."

"Oh," she said, leaning forward to straighten the table-cloth and show him some cleavage. "Well, I can understand that a big man like you probably has a few enemies along with admirers. And you may count me among the latter. I saw what you did to Marshal Haggerty."

"Thanks," Longarm said, thinking that, under completely different circumstances, he would be inclined to develop more than a passing acquaintance with this bold girl.

"You just holler, Marshal, if you need any little thing," she said, moving off and swinging her shapely hips.

Longarm shook his head and dug into his breakfast. He made short work of the biscuits and the gravy, and even enjoyed the steak, although he figured it must have been chiseled off the south end of a Mexican mule. After about three cups of coffee, he knew that it was time to get to moving. Prescott was starting to come alive and Longarm was in a hurry to make his arrest.

He rode out of town while the sun was still climbing on the horizon, and was trotting across Hal Brodie's ranch yard before ten o'clock in the morning.

131

"Hello the house!" Longarm called.

No one answered, but a cowboy emerged from the barn. He stared at Longarm a moment before recognizing him, and said, "Marshal Long. How are you?"

"I'm fine. Lookin' for your boss. Is he around?"

"Nope."

"Where can I find him?"

"Mr. Brodie is over to the Ortega ranch. Went two days ago and hasn't come back yet."

"I see." Longarm forced a smile. "Thanks. I'll just ride over there."

"I'm sure he'll be glad to see you," the cowboy said, acting friendly. "By the way, whatever happened to Mrs. Ortega? Did she go to prison?"

"No," Longarm said, reining his horse around and setting it to a gallop.

Since the Ortega and the Brodie ranches were neighbors, it did not take more than forty minutes for Longarm to arrive at Don Luis's old rancho. There were horses in the corral and, when Longarm appeared, a fair amount of activity.

"Good morning," a ranch hand said as he looked up from working on a broken corral fence.

"Morning," Longarm said. "Is Mr. Brodie staying here?"

"He sure is. Ought to be inside. Probably still having breakfast with Señor Ortega."

That would be Don Luis's brother.

"Thanks," Longarm said, riding over to a hitching rail and dismounting.

He went up to the door of the ranch house and knocked loudly. A man answered the door.

"Señor?"

"I'd like to see Mr. Brodie."

"This way, *por favor*."

Longarm followed the man into the house and down a tiled corridor to a big dining room where Hal Brodie was, indeed, having breakfast with Don Luis's brother.

"Marshal!" Brodie exclaimed, his fork falling from his hand to clatter on his plate. "What a . . . a surprise!"

"I'm sure that it is."

Brodie glanced at the man who had brought Longarm in. "Marshal, this is Miguel Rivera," he said with emphasis.

Longarm nodded and said nothing.

"How . . . how is Lucy?" Brodie stammered, recovering from his surprise. "I've been so worried about her!"

"And that's probably why you've been staying here instead of at your own ranch, huh?"

Brodie was thrown off balance. "What do you mean?"

Longarm saw no point in further conversation. He walked over to Brodie and drew his six-gun. "I'm putting you under arrest for the murder of Don Luis."

"What!"

Juan Ortega, who had been about to take a sip of coffee, dropped his hand to the table, spilling the coffee. He started to come to his feet, but Longarm's words stopped him cold.

"Ortega, I don't know if you and those other two relatives were in cahoots with Brodie or not. Until I do, you'd better stay on this ranch. Understand me?"

Ortega was not armed. He was a thin man, dark and dangerous-looking, with cruel black eyes. "I think you are making a big mistake," he said, removing a napkin from his shirtfront and slapping it down over his spilled coffee.

"If I am," Longarm said, "I'll live with it. Now, keep your hands up on the table where I can see them. We're leaving and I won't brook any interference."

"This is crazy!" Brodie protested. "I'm not a murderer!"

Longarm jammed his gun into Brodie's spine and prodded him toward the front door. "Just keep your mouth shut and move."

"Are you taking me to jail?"

"Not here in Prescott," Longarm said, "where you can have your friend Haggerty set you free the minute I turn my back. No, sir, we're on our way to Yuma."

"Yuma! This is insane! Are you out of your mind, Marshal!"

"Nope. I think we've finally got this thing sorted out as to who really killed Don Luis. It was you, Hal."

"You *are* insane!"

"Maybe," Longarm said, jabbing the man hard in the spine and propelling him toward the door. "But we can let a jury make that determination."

"I'm not going to Yuma!"

"The hell you say," Longarm gritted. "And when we get there, you can see Lucy and tell her yourself how you murdered her husband and tried to get Maria Escobar to lie about it."

"What?"

Longarm caught sight of Miguel Rivera, the cook, and said, "I expect you haven't a clue as to what was in store for you, Rivera, but you were going to take the fall for the murder of Don Luis."

The cook just blinked, not really comprehending. Longarm didn't care. He shoved Brodie out the door and into the yard. "Let's find you a horse and ride."

Brodie looked around wildly for help and, seeing none, he stammered, "If Maria said that she saw me kill Don Luis, *she's* lying!"

"I don't think so."

"It'll just be her word against mine. That won't stand up in any court!"

"I think it will," Longarm said. "You had the motive and the means. You had everything to gain by killing Don Luis—his wife and his ranch. What would Maria stand to gain by lying?"

"She's blackmailing me!"

"Tell it to a jury." Longarm shoved Brodie toward the corral. "Saddle and bridle your horse. We're getting out of here."

Brodie looked around wildly, and then he shouted. "Juan! Manuel! Renaldo! Someone help me!"

"No one is going to help you," Longarm said. "Now grab a bridle and a horse!"

But Brodie wasn't listening. He spun around toward the house. "If you don't help me, I'll tell them everything!"

Longarm took two quick steps and brought the heavy barrel of his pistol crashing down across Brodie's skull. The man's eyes rolled up into his skull and he collapsed.

Longarm took a bridle and went into the corral. There were five horses and he knew that the chestnut belonged to Brodie, so he bridled the animal and led it over to the tack room, where he found a saddle. In minutes he had the chestnut saddled, and then he led it back to the unconscious rancher.

"By the time you come around," he said, holstering his gun so that he could drag Brodie to his feet, "we'll be halfway to Wickenburg."

Longarm heaved Brodie up across his saddle and tied him down with a lariat. Then he got his own horse and mounted, keeping an eye on the ranch house. He did

135

not know if Don Luis's worthless relatives were in on this murder, but he suspected that they might be. Maybe Brodie would carry out his threat, in which case the three would be arrested as accomplices to murder.

But that was something that would have to be faced later.

Longarm rode out of the yard at a trot, leading Brodie's horse with its rider draped unconscious across his saddle. It was another forty miles back down to Wickenburg and Longarm was getting mighty weary of the trip, but he was also satisfied that justice was finally being carried out.

"You're going to either hang or you're going to spend the rest of your natural life in the Yuma Territorial Prison," he told the unconscious rancher as they trotted south.

Chapter 15

"You'll never make this stick," Hal Brodie snarled as they rode down the muddy mountainside in a heavy rain. "And Marshal, before I'm finished, I'm going to make you sorry for the day you were born."

Longarm had tied the man's hands behind his back and his boots to his stirrups. He was leading Brodie's chestnut by a rope tied fast around his own saddlehorn. They were slowly descending a steep grade and, because of the rain, the footing was extremely treacherous and sloppy with mud. Off to his right stretched a vast gorge, and the drop-off from the road was at least two hundred feet almost straight down the mountainside. Every quarter hour or so, they would meet a wagon churning mud up the steep grade. The poor horses would be slipping and clawing for footing, and the road was corkscrewed and dangerous even under the best of conditions.

Longarm pulled his hat down low over his eyes. It didn't rain a whole hell of a lot in Arizona, but when it did, it really poured. "Why don't you save your breath," Longarm said cryptically. "Tell Judge Benton about how you're going to get even with a United States deputy marshal. That will impress the hell out of him."

"You've got nothing on me but the word of a Mexican maid. A nobody!"

"If I have to," Longarm said, "I'll come back to Prescott and shake the truth out of Don Luis's relatives. I expect that they figured to cash in almost as much as you."

Brodie cursed and stammered, "You're just barking up the wrong tree."

"I don't think so," Longarm said, "and neither did Judge Benton when he instructed me to come and arrest you."

"He did that?" Brodie asked, clearly stunned.

"You bet he did." Longarm couldn't help but smile. "The judge believes Maria and so will a jury."

Brodie fell into a brooding silence. He was no longer the handsome, debonair fellow he'd been when Longarm had first met him. Now he was sullen, and sat hunched over in his saddle as they endured the rain.

"Damn," Longarm swore, peering ahead. "Another wagon."

It was a big, high-sided freight wagon and it was hogging the center of the road, just like most of the others had done when Longarm had been forced to ride far over to the side.

"Hey!" Longarm shouted angrily as the wagon grew nearer. "Move over!"

But the driver's hat was pulled far down over his eyes and his head was bent low. Off to the east, thunder rolled and lightning cracked. Longarm guessed he had not been so wet, cold, and miserable in a good long while.

"Hey, dammit! Pull over!"

Suddenly, the driver did pull over, but to the high side of the road. Longarm had no choice but to rein his horse and go to the downside. He wasn't a bit happy as the freight wagon started to brush past, and he meant to give the driver a good piece of his mind. "You stupid . . ."

Longarm's insult died on his lips as the driver sawed on his reins and the front wheel of his wagon veered sharply toward Longarm and his mount. He tried to spur his horse past the big freight wagon, but there just wasn't time as Brodie's chestnut panicked and attempted to whirl.

Longarm heard Brodie scream as his chestnut's hindquarters dropped over the edge of the cliff. For a terrible instant, the chestnut clawed with its forelegs and Brodie tried to unload, but he was tied to his stirrups and helpless.

Longarm heard Brodie scream, "No! God, no!"

And then the man's horse vanished. Longarm instinctively reached for the lead lope attached to his saddlehorn, but there wasn't nearly enough time to untie it. His own stout gelding planted its hooves in the mud and tried to fight the terrible weight that was dragging it over the side of the mountain, but the mud was just too slick to get purchase, and Longarm felt his horse being yanked right over the edge of the cliff.

There was nothing for Longarm to do but bail out of his saddle, and that was when two riflemen opened fire from the back of the passing freight wagon. Longarm heard a bullet whip-crack past his ear, and then he was tumbling over the cliff along with Brodie and their horses.

Longarm kicked out of his stirrups. He struck a boulder and then crashed into a small pine tree jutting out from the side of the mountain at a forty-five-degree angle. In a desperate attempt to keep from plunging to his death, Longarm clamped a fist on the tree and managed to arrest his fall. He glanced downward to see Brodie and their horses tumbling wildly down the mountainside. Longarm knew they were all dead long before they plummeted to the rocks far below where a stream ran full with muddy rainwater.

It had all happened so suddenly that Longarm was dazed. He pounded the toes of his boots into the crumbling mountainside and found purchase. Hanging onto the pine tree, which was about four feet tall and jutting out from the side of the mountain, Longarm knew that he was all but invisible from up on the road even though it was only about thirty feet overhead.

Longarm's face was numb, and he had to blink both blood and rain from his eyes. He hooked his left arm tightly around the trunk of the tree, batting branches and pine needles out of his eyes. He was covered with mud, his clothes torn and twisted around his body. But when he reached down to his side with his right hand, he found that he still had his six-gun jammed deep into his holster.

Longarm heard shouted voices from up above. He drew his six-gun, peered through the pine needles, and saw Juan Ortega and two other men who he figured were Don Luis's other relatives starting down through the driving rain toward the rocks far below. With thunder rolling across the mountain and rain pelting his scratched and bruised face, Longarm couldn't hear what the three were saying, but they were definitely excited. They kept pointing and squinting, probably trying to locate human bodies somewhere on the canyon floor.

Longarm cocked back the hammer of his gun. The three relatives of the late Don Luis had given neither him nor Brodie any chance to survive, and Longarm knew they'd kill him in a heartbeat if they happened to see him hanging from this pine tree, helplessly exposed to their fire. That was why Longarm knew that he could not afford to hope that they would not see him. After all, they showed no sign of leaving the edge of the road above until they were well satisfied that both their intended victims were dead. In fact, one of them actually came over the lip of the road and down a few yards, despite the warnings of his excited companions.

Longarm wiped his eyes clear with the back of his soggy sleeve, and then he took a deep breath and began to fire as rapidly as he could. His first bullet hit the first man dead-center in the chest, and he howled and pitched forward, doing a complete somersault. He struck the side of the mountain not ten feet from Longarm, bounced like a ball, and went careening end over end down the slope. The second man was the recipient of Longarm's second slug, and it caught him in the groin. He collapsed to his knees screaming in agony. Longarm knew he wasn't going anywhere, but Juan Ortega, the man with the cruel eyes, was quick enough to disappear before Longarm could get off a clean shot.

"Damn!" Longarm swore, knowing that Ortega would escape before there was any chance of killing the man.

Meanwhile, the second man was trying to drag his gun up and fire down at Longarm, but he was in too much pain. He cursed at the sky and fired into the dirt while Longarm holstered his six-gun and struggled to pull himself up and over the pine tree. Somehow, he did. Clawing and scrambling and tearing at rock and mud, he crawled up the mountainside using every handhold he could find, and some that didn't appear to exist.

The wounded man, eyes glazing with death, watched him and kept trying to pick up his gun. But he was in such intense agony that his body would not obey his mind, and so he watched helplessly as Longarm finally scrambled over the edge of the cliff and rolled upon his back, chest heaving for breath.

Ortega was nowhere in sight, but Longarm could hear his fading shouts as he whipped one of the wagon team's horses on up the mountain road as fast as it could lumber through the muck. No matter, Longarm thought. The road to Denver, Colorado, leads back through Prescott and I'll find Don Luis's scheming brother somewhere.

The wounded man slowly twisted around to face Longarm. He gripped his right wrist with his left hand and, with his fading strength, managed to raise his six-gun a few precious inches.

"Hold it," Longarm panted, yanking out his own gun and leveling it at the man. "Just drop the gun."

He wasn't going to do it. The gun was like a terrible weight in his hands, and his determination was heroic as he slowly raised it by fractions of an inch.

Longarm waited an instant longer, and then he put a bullet through the man's brain. He was rocked backward, and tumbled over the side of the cliff.

Longarm wasn't sure how long he lay gasping for breath with the rain washing the mud and blood from his eyes. Maybe it was a half hour, perhaps much longer. But finally, he pushed himself to his feet. The saddle horses were gone, as was his prisoner. His saddle, rifle, bedroll, and saddlebags were all crushed under what was left of his poor horse lying far below.

"Shit," Longarm swore as he pushed himself to his feet and slogged through mud over to the freight wagon.

He had a pocketknife, and used it to cut one of the team horses free. Then he mounted the animal, plow-reined it around, and continued on down the hill toward Wickenburg.

He had only gone a mile when he came upon a dead man lying face-down in the mud of the road. Longarm did not have to puzzle about the man's identity, because he knew it had to be the driver of the freight wagon who had met this sad end at the hands of the three Mexicans.

Longarm slid down from the draft horse and went over to turn the freighter over onto his back. The fellow had been shot right between the eyes. He'd probably never known what hit him, and he'd most certainly had no warning.

Longarm dragged the body as far as he could off the road, feeling bitterness and anger rising in his throat. This man had not deserved to die. He hadn't done any-thing except be unfortunate enough to have a wagon that the Mexicans wanted in order to knock both Longarm and his prisoner to their deaths far below in the canyon.

Longarm searched the man for some identification, but found none. They had emptied his pockets. He looked to have been a young man, probably no more than thirty years old. It was a damn, crying shame.

"Mister," Longarm said, squatting on his heels in the rain. "It started with Don Luis, and now it's ending with a couple of his dead relatives, that snake Hal Brodie, and finally you."

Longarm came to his feet. "I promise that I'll get someone up here to move you just as soon as I can."

With that simple but seemingly necessary explana-tion completed to the victim, Longarm rode on toward

143

Wickenburg and a stagecoach that would carry him back to Yuma to wrap up this tragic series of murders.

Before he had gone a mile, Longarm met another freight wagon. He reined his wagon horse directly into the wagon's path, forcing the driver to pull up short.

"Hey!" the driver yelled. "Don't you know how tough it is for these horses when you break a wagon's momentum?"

"I can appreciate that," Longarm said, dragging out his badge and showing it to the man. "I'm a United States marshal and there's a dead freighter lying beside the road just a short ways up ahead."

"You kill him?"

"No," Longarm said. "He was murdered by three men who tried to knock me over the side of this mountain. They halfway succeeded."

"You look like you been crawlin' in a swamp and whipped most to death, Marshal. You look real bad."

"I'm alive," Longarm said. "I wish that I could say the same thing for the young driver that was murdered. How about picking him up and taking him on to Prescott?"

"Sure. Any idea who he is?"

"No," Longarm said. "But I'm sure that someone will be able to identify him and notify his next of kin."

"What about them three that ambushed you?"

"Two are dead but one escaped. I'll be back for him later."

"You tell me who it was, I'll get some of us freighters together and we'll settle the score."

"I wish that I could let you do that," Longarm said. "But I can't. It's my job, and I'll take care of it when I return from Yuma."

"Probably ain't even rainin' down there in Yuma," the driver said, looking grim. "This damn weather makes this road a gutter of mud and they don't pay me enough to drive a freight wagon at times like this."

"I can appreciate that," Longarm said. "Just pick up that body and take it into Prescott."

"I guess you'll want me to notify Marshal Haggerty," the driver said.

"I'm sure that he'll find out. Tell him that Marshal Long will be coming back through to sort out the pieces."

"He ain't going to be too happy waitin' until then."

"Don't mean a damn to me if he's happy or not," Longarm said abruptly. "Just get the body to the under-taker."

"You or the government payin' for his burial?"

"Sorry," Longarm said, "but I'm about broke. Take up a collection. Okay?"

"Sure." The driver pulled his hat down a little lower, and then he spat a stream of tobacco juice into the mud. "No, sir, they don't pay me near enough to drive in this kind of sloppy shit!"

Longarm reined his draft horse aside and the wagon passed. He wiped his face with his sleeve and clenched his teeth to keep them from chattering. It was still, he guessed, about twenty miles to Wickenburg and it was going to be a long, slow ride.

Chapter 16

By the time he reached Wickenburg, Longarm was a sick and miserable dog. He was sneezing and his nose was running. He felt feverish, and decided that he had better get a hotel room and get to bed before he contracted pneumonia, an affliction that killed almost as many men in the West as did bullets.

He called for a doctor and went straight to bed.

"Marshal," the doctor said a short time later, "you're in pretty poor shape. You're underweight for a man your height and frame and your lungs sound like a bubbling brook. I'm going to give you some medicine and you're going to have to stay put for a couple of weeks."

"A couple of days," Longarm said before breaking into a fit of prolonged coughing.

When he was able to stop, the doctor produced a bottle of Dr. Ormly's Cough Elixir and Restorative. Longarm frowned. "I never heard of this stuff. Who the hell is Dr. Ormly?"

"Beats me," the doctor said. "But the damned stuff seems to work. It's got some tar and licorice in it for the taste, some pure-grain alcohol, and some 'Indian healing herbs' according to the label. All I know is that it tastes good, it makes you feel a whole lot better, and it'll kill that nasty cough."

"I'll take about three bottles," Longarm said. "Money is in my pants pocket."

"You're going to need someone to bring you food and take care of your needs," the doctor said. "I'll be checking with you at least three times a day until you stop feeling feverish and your lungs clear up so that you can take a deep breath without drowning."

"Do you have someone in mind?"

"There's the Widow Wallace," the doctor said, "but she's pretty damned bossy and she looks like she ought to be runnin' a prison chain gang. I will say she's strong and willing."

"Well, I'm not willing," Longarm said. "Anybody else?"

"Mrs. Anastopolos is kinder, but she's Greek and doesn't speak very good English. Mrs. Chang is Chinese and—"

"She doesn't speak good English either."

"Yeah," the doctor countered, "but you're not going to be much for talking until that sore throat starts to feeling better."

"True," Longarm agree, "but I thought that Dr. Ormly's medicine would take care of that."

"In a few days, if we're lucky."

Longarm pointed a finger at the man. "Dr. Hubbard, luck hasn't got much to do with this. I'm counting on you to pull me through. I've got to get back to Yuma."

"Excellent climate for what ails you," Hubbard said with a tired grin. "And I suppose that you've been in so many gunfights that the idea of dying of pneumonia must surely take some getting used to."

"I'm not going to die," Longarm said, realizing that Hubbard was teasing him in order to lift his low spirits. "But isn't there anyone more . . . personable who wouldn't mind bringing up my meals?"

"Well, there is that new girl who is working at the Sagebrush Cafe. She's short, only about five feet tall, but fills out her blouse about as well as a man could hope to see. Her name is Willa. Willa Handover."

"Does she act married or engaged?"

"She isn't," the doctor said, "but she's got every bachelor in Wickenburg eating out of her hand."

"Do you think that she'd be willing to bring my meals up here?"

"I doubt it," Hubbard said. "But I enjoy being served by Willa as much as the next red-blooded American male. I'll ask her tonight when I have supper there."

"You don't eat at home?"

"My wife of twenty-three years died last summer," the doctor said, his grin fading, "*of pneumonia* not much worse than yours. But she wasn't nearly as young or as strong."

"I'm sorry," Longarm said, meaning it. He had liked Dr. Hubbard from the first moment the man had entered his hotel room and jammed a thermometer into his mouth.

"Here," the doctor said, pulling a couple of bottles of the elixir out of his medical kit and opening one. To Longarm's surprise and amusement, he upended the bottle and took a sample for himself.

"Yep, Marshal, it's the right stuff."

"Was there any doubt?"

"There isn't now," Hubbard said with a wink as he snapped his bag shut and eased off the hotel bed. "Got to go now."

"Will I see you after supper?"

"Yep."

Longarm took a long slug of the bottle and smacked his lips. The medicine was good. "Better give me a couple of extra bottles," he said.

"Better give me some cash."

"Pants pocket, Doc."

Hubbard pulled out the last of Longarm's cash and counted it solemnly. Looking up, he said, "Doesn't the government pay you fellas enough money to do your job?"

"This trip has been a lot more expensive than any of us back in Denver expected. Would it be too much to ask you to wire my boss, Marshal Billy Vail, for some extra cash and to let him know what I'm up to?"

"I'd be happy to do that."

"I don't suppose you have paper and pencil on you?"

"I do," the doctor said.

Longarm didn't feel much like writing Billy a telegraph message, but he knew that one was long overdue so he scribbled, "Billy, Send more money. Pneumonia in Wickenburg but will recover shortly. Mrs. Ortega cleared and safe in Yuma. Will arrive there next week. Send a hundred dollars."

The doctor read the telegraph message and raised his eyebrows. "You are definitely too optimistic about getting out of this bed next week. But I like the sound of the hundred dollars. It ought to cover my fees quite nicely."

"Like hell," Longarm said, breaking into another fit of coughing that nearly doubled him up in his bed.

Dr. Hubbard patted Longarm's shoulder and quickly left him to his private misery. Longarm upended the bottle of elixir, and sighed as the sweet but fiery medicine trickled down his ravaged throat. He sneezed and blew his nose and groaned.

"Sonofabitch," he croaked, "I don't need this kind of grief."

He must have fallen asleep, because it was dark outside his window when the doctor, whom he'd given a key to his hotel room, knocked and then opened the door.

"Marshal, have you died yet?"

Longarm jerked into wakefulness. He felt a little better, he guessed. "No such luck, Doc."

"Then I guess you'll want Willa to bring up some supper after all. Something soft to swallow for that sore throat."

"She's going to do it?"

"I told her I sent a telegraph to Denver asking for a hundred dollars expense money. I take it that she is going to consider herself a big expense. About like me."

"I'd be willing to pay her a whole lot more than you," Longarm said, forcing a smile.

Hubbard sat down beside him on the bed and turned up the wick to his bedside lamp. He produced a thermometer and Longarm dutifully opened his mouth. "I hope you washed the damn thing this time."

"Not since I shoved it up Abe Benford's ass," the doctor said without cracking a smile as he jammed the thermometer between Longarm's teeth.

Longarm started to chuckle, but that caused his throat to ache, so he just lay still and suffered in silence until

Hubbard removed the thermometer and eyed it critically.

"Temperature is still about a hundred and two," he said. "But that's not going to fry your brains."

"What brains I have left."

"I'm glad you said that and not me," the doctor told him as he pulled out his stethoscope and rechecked Longarm's lungs, saying, "I'm sure you realize that I'd rather do this with Miss Handover."

"Goes without saying, Doc."

"Cough."

Longarm coughed.

"Sounds awful."

"Thanks for the encouraging words."

Hubbard stood up and put away his instruments. He glanced over his shoulder at the door. "I told the cook over at the Sagebrush Cafe that I wanted you to eat a lot, but nothing that was going to aggravate your sore throat."

"Good. How long until Willa arrives?"

"Ten or fifteen minutes, but you sure don't look like any prize with your face all scratched up."

Longarm turned his lamp down low. "Better?"

"Turn it out and it would be even better yet."

"Once Willa gets here and I've had my supper, I'll try to get her to help me do that," Longarm said, knowing that he was bluffing and in no condition to do much more than lie still and breathe.

"In your pitiful condition, a woman like Willa would send you to an early grave."

Longarm suspected that the doctor was only half serious, and so he clamped his mouth shut and resolved to stop the banter.

"Nothing but food, lots of liquids, and rest," Hubbard warned as he headed for the door again.

"Be sure and lock it on your way out," Longarm croaked.

"What's the matter, having second thoughts about Willa?"

"Nope, but a man in my line of work makes a lot of enemies over the years," Longarm explained. "And I just don't feel up to killing any bad men today."

"Understandable," Hubbard said. "Willa can get her key at the front desk."

Longarm thought that was just fine. He drank a little more elixir, turned down the bedside lamp even lower, smoothed his hair, and wished he felt up to a shave and a bath. He was a dirty mess, with mud still caked in his hair and the creases of his skin. No doubt about it, Willa Handover wasn't going to be dazzled by his pitiful appearance.

She arrived in fifteen minutes, just like Dr. Hubbard had predicted, and the moment Willa sashayed into his room, Longarm felt a whole lot better.

"Marshal Long," she said, setting a big tray of steaming food down on his bed, "you look awful."

"I feel even worse."

Willa's soft, warm fingers touched his bruised and battered cheek. "I'm going to help you feel better, Marshal."

"For the money?"

She laughed. "Partly, but also because my father was a lawman and he was the finest person that ever walked the streets of Tucson, Arizona."

"I see."

Willa leaned forward and kissed Longarm on the forehead. "You're burning up and it isn't with desire for me."

"It could be."

"Not a chance," she told him as she got a napkin out and spread it across his raspy chest. "Now, we'll start with the vegetable soup with bread, not crackers."

"Sounds good."

"And then we've got some beef stew, and we'll finish up with some vanilla pudding. How does that sound?"

"Everything you say sounds good."

She laughed. A nice, throaty, sexy laugh. Longarm felt like laughing too, only he knew better than to try. "Tell me all about you," he said as she dipped a spoon into the vegetable soup and brought it to his lips.

"I'm a girl who likes strong and wealthy men."

Longarm took a gulp of the soup. It was excellent. "I'm neither."

"You're at least strong," Willa said, looking into his eyes. "And as for the wealth, well, a girl can't have everything."

"I sure am glad you're not the Widow Wallace," Longarm whispered.

She gave him a quizzical look and then kept the soup coming.

Chapter 17

Longarm wrapped himself in Willa, his body thrusting mightily as the young woman moaned under his weight, breasts heaving as if she had climbed some great mountain. When Willa began to cry out with passion, Longarm covered her sweet lips with his own and then their bodies stiffened, fire coursing into fire.

"Oh," Willa gasped, "I can't get enough of you, Marshal."

"You're wearing me down to the bone," he said with a smile. "You seem to have forgotten that I'm a sick man."

"Yeah, sure," she said, hugging him tightly. "If you were completely healthy I think you might have put me in my grave, but I'd be there with a smile on my face."

Longarm chuckled. "I don't know how to thank you for taking care of me this past week. I wish I didn't have to board that stagecoach this morning, but I've no choice."

"I know," she said. "But you'll be back through, won't you?"

Longarm's answer was hesitant. "I might, but I can't be certain. My original orders were to return a bunch of prisoners to Denver."

"Why won't they let you have a few weeks of vacation with me?" Willa asked. "You need rest."

"You're not giving me much."

"I did the first day. You were in bad shape when I came to visit you the first time."

"I suppose that I was. Dr. Hubbard kept looking at me like I had one foot in the grave. He was pretty relieved when I got that hundred dollars of expense money from Denver."

"Dr. Hubbard barely makes a living. People pay him with milk, eggs, butter, chickens, and about everything except cash. He needed your government money, Custis."

"What about you?" Longarm gazed into her blue eyes. "Willa, you haven't asked me for a cent."

"No," she said with a smile, "not yet."

"I'm giving you fifty dollars," he decided out loud. "I know you've lost wages and tips because you've spent so much time with me this past week."

"Thanks. It was a pleasure."

"I've got to go," Longarm said, pushing off of her warm, soft body and pausing to admire it one last time. "No man ever had a better nurse."

"Any time," she said, enjoying the admiration she saw reflected in his eyes. "Any old time."

Longarm dressed quickly and strapped on his gunbelt. His lips raised in a slight smile and he said, "My belt is one notch farther out, thanks to your cooking."

"You're still too skinny," she told him. "You could use another twenty pounds, easy."

"I guess."

"And I could put them on you in about two weeks, if things change and you find you can stop over for a while on your way back from Yuma."

"Not likely, but I'll keep it in mind. Besides, for every two pounds I gain, I work one of 'em off in bed with you, Willa."

She giggled, but when he came over to kiss her good-bye, her eyes were shining with tears and she hugged his neck tightly, not wanting to let him go.

"Time for us both to get back to work, Willa," he said, feeling his own throat lump. "Time for me to climb on that early morning stage to Yuma."

She took a deep breath and said, "And I guess I ought to go back to the Sagebrush Cafe and serve breakfast."

Longarm slipped fifty dollars into her dress pocket and blew Willa a kiss good-bye. He had already paid Dr. Hubbard, which did not leave him much cash. But he had sold both his horse and Lucy's strawberry roan for a pretty good price, so he knew that he would be just fine.

"Back to Yuma, huh, Marshal?" the driver said fifteen minutes later as Longarm pitched his saddlebags and bedroll inside.

"That's right."

"Well, we've only got two other passengers to keep you company today. The Reverend Bertram B. Cheshire and his wife, Agnes. They'll keep you awake."

Longarm glanced inside the stage. It was still empty, meaning the reverend and his wife had not yet arrived. "What does that mean?"

"Are you a churchgoin' man?"

"I go to weddings and funerals."

"Well," the driver said with a wink, "you'll sure hear the word of God. I expect that old Bertram will want to put the fire of redemption in your soul."

Longarm expelled a deep breath. "Thanks for the warning," he said, climbing into the coach and wanting nothing better than to rest quietly as this stagecoach carried him back to Yuma.

"They're real nice people," the driver said. "Agnes can get a little tedious, but she's probably got a picnic basket packed with food, and they're both generous people."

"Glad to hear that."

"But don't be carrying whiskey and takin' snorts in their presence," the driver warned. "Both Bert and Agnes are just death on drink."

"I haven't any whiskey," Custis said. "But it sounds as if maybe I should buy a bottle. Perhaps that way they'd write me off and leave me in peace to rest."

"Doubt it," the driver said, "but if you did that, you'd miss out on the picnic basket."

"Life is full of hard choices," Longarm said, climbing inside and taking his seat.

Five minutes later, the reverend and his wife appeared. He was a little man, bald with round spectacles and a slight hitch in his gait. Longarm judged the reverend to be in his mid-sixties, and despite his slight limp and diminutive size, he looked lively and cheerful. Agnes was quite his opposite. She was a very large woman. Agnes dwarfed her husband and wore a shapeless print dress, pink crocheted sweater, and her shoes were so tight the tops of her feet sort of puffed out. She looked crabby and critical to Longarm, and her brows were knitted in disapproval. Longarm could see right away that Agnes would take up the entire bench, while he and the reverend would be forced to share the opposite seat. It was, he thought, a good thing that there were only the three of them traveling down to Yuma.

"My dear, let me help you up," the reverend said, giving Longarm a glance.

"You can't help me," Agnes complained. "I need a strong man."

She looked into the coach, sizing Longarm up and then snapping, "What about you, young man?"

"I'm not in good health," Longarm said, not at all wanting to try to boost Agnes up and through the stagecoach door. "Why don't you ask the stationmaster if he's got a box or a ladder that you can climb onto?"

"Humph!" Agnes snorted, clearly displeased with a suggestion that Longarm thought entirely sensible.

"I think that would be a good idea," the reverend said cautiously.

"Very well! Find a ladder, Bertram!"

"I'll get you something," the driver promised. "We've got a big stepping box that comes in handy once in a while."

Agnes colored a little because the driver's implication was that she was among a very few passengers who were either too fat or too infirm to get into the coach without extraordinary measures being taken in their behalf.

In a few moments, two of the stage line employees were dragging a heavy wooden structure that was built so sturdily out of two-by-sixes that it would have supported a milk cow.

"There you go, Agnes," the reverend said. "Ladies first!"

Longarm felt the entire coach lurch on its leather straps when Agnes stepped on board. The big, sour-faced woman almost lost her balance, and might have tumbled back out the door and crushed her husband if Longarm hadn't grabbed her chubby wrist and hauled her the rest of the way inside.

"Easy now," he said as she collapsed on her side of the coach.

"Don't 'easy now' me! You sound as if you're talking to a horse instead of a lady."

"Sorry, ma'am."

"He meant no offense," the reverend said as he spryly hopped up the loading ramp and popped onto the seat beside Longarm. "Agnes, this is the legendary Deputy Marshal Custis Long."

"Yes," she snapped, "the one that killed all those men on the road to Prescott and that has been sleeping with that tramp Willa Handover! You're going to burn in hell, Marshal!"

"Agnes!"

Longarm bristled and looked to the reverend. "I remember a few passages from the Holy Bible and one of 'em says, 'Judge not lest ye be judged.' It seems that your wife has forgotten that bit of the gospel."

Even in the dim interior of the coach, Longarm could see the way that Agnes swelled up in anger like a scalded toad while her husband seemed to shrink into the seat cushions.

"He's right, Agnes. We should not judge the sinner lest we be judged by the Lord for our own sins."

"Shut up and save it for the pulpit, Mr. Cheshire. I don't appreciate having to travel with this . . . this wretched sinner."

Longarm had heard about enough. It was all that he could do to bite his tongue and exit the coach.

"I'm riding up top with you," he said, climbing up to join the driver.

"You're going to miss out on some good food."

"It'll be worth it," Longarm said, "just to breath some clean air."

The driver nodded with understanding. "I didn't think you'd last very long down there with Agnes, but I figured we'd at least get out of Wickenburg before you come up from down below."

"Well," Longarm said, jamming a cheroot between his teeth, "you figured wrong. Now let's go!"

The driver snapped his whip and the stage rolled out of town. Longarm was still so riled that he chewed his cheroot right down to a nub before they'd gone a mile.

Chapter 18

When Longarm finally returned to Yuma, he went straight to see Judge Harvey Benton and found the man presiding over his court. Longarm cooled his heels in the hallway for almost an hour before the bailiff led a disreputable-looking man out wearing a pair of handcuffs.

"Yuma Prison for drunk and disorderly!" the prisoner wailed. "My God, what kind of justice is that!"

"It's the kind of justice that repeat offenders like you will get in his court," the bailiff said without a hint of sympathy. "What do you expect? This is the fifth time you've been hauled in here in the last two months."

"But . . . but I didn't get drunk for three days straight this time! And I didn't steal but five dollars and change."

"Well," the bailiff said as they marched down the hallway, "I guess you'll have plenty of time to sober up and change your ways. A year in prison might be the best thing that ever happened to you."

"It'll *kill* me is what it'll do!"

"No, it won't," the bailiff said. "People come out of there a whole hell of a lot healthier than when they come in. Lighter, sure, but also healthier."

"Oh, God!"

Longarm shook his head. He couldn't muster up much sympathy for the prisoner because a thief was a thief. Furthermore, Longarm had seen too damn many drunks go on rampages and kill innocent people. When honest men got drunk, they stayed honest, but a bad one always showed his true colors.

Longarm stepped into the judge's quarters. "Judge Benton?"

The judge looked up from his bench, and when he saw Longarm he smiled with relief. "I was beginning to wonder what happened to you, Marshal."

"Well," Longarm said, "I had some problems."

"I'm listening."

Longarm told the judge about how he'd arrested Hal Brodie for the murder of Lucy's husband. "Of course, he strenuously objected and even threatened me, saying that it was just his word against that of the Mexican girl."

"I'm sure he'll be convicted and sentenced," the judge said, "But where is the man?"

Longarm told Benton about the surprise attack on the muddy and slippery road leading down from Prescott to Wickenburg and how Brodie had plunged to his death.

"But I was lucky enough to kill Padilla and Lopez. Juan Ortega, Don Luis's brother, escaped, but I should be able to find him on my way back through Prescott."

"I'm afraid," the judge said, "that you're still going to have to take our female prisoners to Colorado."

Longarm almost burst a blood vessel. "Judge, haven't I got enough trouble without having to nursemaid a bunch of women back to Colorado!"

"Yes," Benton said sympathetically, "you most certainly have. But these prisoners *have* to be transported to Denver by a federal marshal."

"But Judge, I—"

"I'm going to reduce the number of prisoners from one dozen to ten, and I'll assign you two excellent Arizona prison guards to help you. I promise, the task will not be difficult or dangerous."

"Any time you have custody of women, things get complicated," Longarm said angrily. "And don't forget, I'll need to find and arrest Ortega."

"Yes," the judge said, "and I know you'll do that without great difficulty. But before you leave Yuma, you must take custody of the ten women prisoners and deliver them to Denver. I've been in touch with your Denver office. A Marshal William Vail. We've exchanged several telegrams and he has assured me that you are the ideal candidate for this job."

"Excuse my French," Longarm growled, "but that's just pure horseshit."

Benton's eyebrows knitted. "Marshal," he said sternly, "you've been ordered to perform an important job and you will do it. Perhaps not very cheerfully, but you will do it."

"Yes, sir."

The judge relaxed. "When would you like to depart with the prison wagon and your charges?"

"Early tomorrow."

"That can be arranged."

Longarm turned to go. He was steamed about this, but there seemed nothing to do but follow orders. Besides, once back in Denver, he'd have three glorious weeks of paid vacation coming and have a wonderful time.

"Marshal Long?"

Longarm stopped at the door and turned. "Yes?"

"I'm going to write a commendation for you and send it to the Governor of Colorado. What you've done for us down here in Arizona is truly remarkable."

"You don't need to do that."

"Of course I don't," Benton said, "but I'm going to anyway. You're a credit to your profession, and that brings me to the sad fact that Marshal Haggerty is probably a discredit to his profession."

Longarm didn't say anything. He didn't like the idea of criticizing a fellow law officer, even one that appeared to be corrupt.

The judge leaned forward, his face very intent as he studied Longarm. "*Is* the marshal in Prescott a discredit to your profession?"

"I don't know," Longarm said truthfully. "I guess, if I can take Juan Ortega alive, I'll make him answer that question."

"If Haggerty was in on this killing, or even if he was just aware of it and failed to carry out justice in the hope of monetary reward, then he needs to be removed him from office at once."

"Yes, sir."

"Good luck, Marshal!"

"I'll need it."

"I don't think so," the judge said. "Men like you don't rely on luck. You're just too good."

Despite his anger, Longarm found himself warmed by the flattery. He bade the judge good-bye, and went to find Lucy and tell her that she was no longer a suspect in the murder of her husband.

• • •

Longarm found Lucy shopping in one of Yuma's better mercantile stores, and when she saw him she let out a squeal of delight and rushed into his arms.

"Custis! Whatever took you so long to return!"

"Come outside and I'll tell you all about it," he said, not wanting to speak about his adventures and near-demise in front of the other customers, who were straining to overhear without being too obvious with their curiosity.

Lucy quickly paid for a few items and they left to walk down the street. When no one could overhear them, Longarm quickly told Lucy about the death of Hal Brodie, Manuel Padilla, and Renaldo Lopez.

"Only Juan Ortega escaped, and I expect I'll find him in Prescott."

"Yes," Lucy agreed. "And I'm coming with you."

"That wouldn't be a good idea," Longarm said, telling her about the ten Yuma Prison female inmates. "I will have to stay with their prison wagon."

"Then I'll go ahead of you."

"No."

"Custis, my home is in Prescott! You can't order me not to return."

"Just . . . just stay here out of harm's way until I arrest or kill Ortega. You can return after that."

Lucy didn't look pleased, but Longarm knew that he was doing the right thing. "It will only be a few days at most," he added. "But to be on the safe side, give it a week."

"I'll give it five days," she decided. "And what about Maria Escobar? Can she return to Prescott?"

"Check with Judge Benton," Longarm said. "But I don't see any reason why she couldn't return with you.

167

Especially since Juan Ortega is the only man who would have any reason for seeing her dead."

"All right," Lucy agreed. "Five days."

"You got any money?" Longarm asked. "I'm low on funds."

"Of course, and I'll buy you supper, after we have a little time together in my hotel room."

"Shameful woman," Longarm said, slipping his arm around Lucy's waist.

She pushed it away and said, "Later."

Longarm grinned because he knew that they would probably be in Lucy's bed within fifteen minutes.

The next morning, Longarm awoke to a knock on Lucy's door. He reached for his six-gun and said, "Who is it?"

"Deputy Jasper Hawkins, Marshal. We got the prison wagon and the wimmen down in the street and we're ready to roll. How come you ain't ready and waitin'?"

Longarm looked at his pocket watch lying on his beside table. He was amazed to see that it was ten o'clock. "Be right down!" he called, rolling out of bed and splashing cold water in his face.

Lucy groaned but did not awaken. They had made love off and on most of the night, and she was probably as exhausted as he was. Longarm decided to let her sleep.

"So long, darlin'. I figure that the next time I see you when I pass through Prescott, you'll be the town's leading lady. Probably have a new husband to take care of your ranch. Maybe have a couple of kids and a good life. At least, I hope that's the way of it."

Longarm felt a little shaky from his recent illness and his long night of lovemaking as he quickly dressed and then packed his bags. But the shakes disappeared when he saw the ten hard-faced women prisoners staring at him through the prison wagon's bars.

Two of them, both big and buxom, whistled derisively when he emerged, and Longarm felt his cheeks warm despite the coolness of the morning.

"Marshal," an older deputy with a hefty paunch and tired brown eyes said, coming forward to extend his hand, "I'm Deputy Prison Supervisor Amos Putterman. I'm in charge of the prisoners, and I guess you've already met my assistant, Deputy Hawkins."

"Yeah," Longarm said.

Putterman made a big show of dragging out his cheap pocket watch, consulting it with a frown, and saying, "We expected to get an *early* start this morning."

"Well," Longarm said, "sometimes things don't always work according to our set schedules."

Putterman didn't like that remark, but Longarm did not care. He climbed up onto the roof of the prison wagon and spread out his bedroll so that he could nap through the morning. The women below began to hoot and shout and bang the ceiling of their wagon, but Longarm was unfazed.

"Let's roll," he said.

The two prison employees climbed up, and Hawkins took the lines while Putterman collected a ten-gauge shotgun, which he cradled across his chubby legs. Just before the wagon lurched forward, Putterman turned and said, "How come we got to pass through Prescott? That's miles out of our way."

"I know," Longarm said. "But I've got business there."

"Your business," Putterman said, "ought to be helping us deliver these noisy bitches to Colorado!"

Longarm took an immediate dislike to Putterman. "They may not be ladies," he said with steel in his voice, "but if I hear you refer to them as bitches or anything other than women, I'll knock your teeth down your throat so far you'll have bite marks on your ass."

Putterman's jaw dropped and he gripped the shotgun so hard his knuckles went white. But he seemed to know better than to say anything, because he turned around and sat in stiff silence.

Longarm stretched out on the top of the prison wagon and his bedroll and watched the clouds scud across the deep indigo sky. It was going to be a fine day, he reminded himself. A fine day followed by a fine week, and they would have a peach of a time on this trip back home to Denver.

"Liar," he muttered to himself.

Chapter 19

"How long are we going to have to wait here?" Putterman demanded.

Longarm levered a shell into his Winchester. He had ordered Putterman to drive the prison wagon into some trees about a half mile from the Ortega ranch house. Far enough that the women couldn't give anyone a warning if they set to howling.

"I expect that I'll be back in less than one hour," Longarm told the man.

"You gonna need some help?" young Hawkins asked hopefully. "If you do, I better come along."

"The hell you say!" Putterman snapped. "Hawkins, you take orders from me, and I'm not about to let you go off on some private feud leaving me alone with these . . . women."

The young prison guard looked crushed, but Longarm was secretly glad that he didn't have to tell Hawkins that he would rather try to take Juan Ortega captive alone.

"Just keep the women under control," Longarm said.

Longarm regretted those words the moment they were out of his mouth. They were overheard by the women, who began to shout and screech like banshees.

"Damn," Longarm said, hoping that they could not be heard from the ranch house.

"Now you've gone and done it," Putterman said with disgust. "Tell 'em they can't do a thing like that and they'll do it to spite you every time."

"So I see," Longarm said, hurrying away.

He could hear the prisoners for the next quarter mile, and then their voices grew faint, and finally they vanished altogether. Longarm circled the ranch house, keeping out of sight. Having been inside before, he felt confident that he could make his way into the house without arousing anyone. He just hoped that Ortega hadn't fled to Mexico. Mainly, Longarm was counting on the man's greed tying him to this ranch.

Longarm came in from behind the house and slipped over the courtyard wall. Moving swiftly past the fountain, he entered the large living room, gun clenched tightly in his fist. He was reminded once again of what a beautiful home this was and how it and Lucy could tempt almost any man to plot and then commit a heinous act of murder.

The first person he saw was another maid, but she did not see him and he waited for her to move on. When she did, Longarm crouched behind a large walnut cabinet and listened to the sound of voices coming from what were probably bedrooms up the hallway.

Juan Ortega's voice was easily recognizable, and Longarm moved swiftly down the hall until he came to Ortega's door. He waited until he heard the voices stop and an inner door open and close, then he opened Ortega's door. The brother of Don Luis was sitting alone at a huge desk, writing furiously when Longarm entered the room.

"You're under arrest, Ortega."

The man stiffened and his hand dropped out of sight. Longarm did not bother to ask what he was reaching for, but shot him in the shoulder. Ortega was seated in a plush leather chair, and the force of Longarm's bullet was so powerful that the front of the chair lifted and the man almost toppled.

Ortega's gun clattered to the tile floor and he cursed fervently as he tried to stop the blood from pouring out of his shoulder.

"Ortega, just put your hands up on the desk where I can see them!"

Ortega placed his left hand on the polished surface of the desk but shook his head. "Marshal, I cannot lift my arm! Your bullet . . ."

Longarm thought the man was probably telling the truth. The slug from his six-gun did appear to have shattered Ortega's shoulder. Longarm walked over, grabbed Ortega by the shirt, and hauled him to his feet.

"You're going to prison," Longarm announced. "You helped Brodie kill your own brother so that you could gain an interest in this land. Then, when you became convinced he would implicate you, you staged that attack on the road down to Wickenburg. You'll be in prison for the rest of your life, Ortega."

The Mexican's lip curled. "If I have to go, I will trade you some information for a lesser sentence."

"What information?"

Ortega's expression turned crafty. "Maybe about another lawman, eh, Marshal?"

Longarm snorted with derision. "No deals."

Ortega was caught by surprise, and his thin lips turned downward with bitterness. "Marshal Long, I'm not going to rot in the Yuma prison while Haggerty gets away free!"

"I suspected Haggerty was somehow a part of this. Are you willing to testify against him without any promises?"

Ortega vigorously nodded his head.

The maid that Longarm had seen earlier appeared with a pistol in her shaking hand. "Señorita," Longarm said, "I am a United States marshal. Put that gun away."

"Your badge, señor?"

Longarm quickly showed her his badge before she accidently shot him. Satisfied, the maid dropped the six-gun.

"I need some bandages," Longarm said. "And hurry."

A few minutes later the maid returned with clean bandages, and Longarm managed to staunch the flow of blood. He tied Ortega's hands loosely behind his back and led him outside.

"Marshal!" the maid cried.

Longarm turned. "What?"

"What am I to do now?"

"Clean and care for the house as usual," Longarm told the frightened woman. "Señora Ortega and Maria Escobar will return very soon."

The maid crossed herself and looked exceedingly happy at this news. Longarm was happy as well.

"Haggerty will kill me if he can," Ortega grated through clenched teeth. "And he'll kill you too."

"He may try," Longarm said, "but he won't succeed."

When Longarm returned to the prison wagon with Ortega, the women prisoners stared through the bars of their wagon at Ortega with great curiosity.

"What are we going to do with him?" Putterman demanded.

"He's a prisoner," Longarm said, "so we'll put him in the wagon."

"With all those women?" Hawkins asked, jaw dropping.

"He's hardly in any shape to take advantage of them." Longarm reminded the young deputy.

"It isn't him that I was thinking about doin' the abusin'," Hawkins said. "*They're* the ones that are going to have the fun with the poor sumbitch."

Longarm shrugged his shoulders and unlocked the door of the prison wagon. When Ortega realized the company he was going to be forced to keep, the pain on his evil face gave way to unbridled panic.

"No, please! Do not put me in there with those whores! I beg you."

"Shouldn't have called them that," Longarm said as the ten women cursed and spat at the wounded Mexican. "I got a feeling that was a *big* mistake."

Ortega renewed his struggles with even more desperation, but all his efforts were to no avail as Longarm forced him into the prison wagon. The women crowded around prodding and poking the terrified Mexican. When Ortega's screams took on a higher pitch, Longarm conceded that he might have made a poor decision. However, he did not think that the women would actually kill Ortega, though some of them were certainly capable of the act.

"Let's go," Longarm said, climbing back onto the roof of the wagon.

"Your new prisoner may be dead by the time we reach Prescott," Putterman said.

"Too bad," Longarm replied, wondering again about a snake who'd had a hand in the murder of his own brother.

Chapter 20

It would have been a pleasant enough journey to Prescott if Juan Ortega had not kept screaming for mercy. Longarm lay stretched out and dozing on his bedroll until Putterman finally pulled the prison wagon to a halt at the edge of town.

"Well, Marshal Long, how do you want to handle this?" the prison supervisor asked.

Longarm sat up and rubbed his eyes, wishing he'd lately gotten more sleep. He yawned and slowly swung his long legs over the side of the wagon.

"Might as well just roll on in and pull up in front of Marshal Haggerty's office. I don't expect he'll try and run."

"What if he decides to shoot it out?" Hawkins asked.

"That's his choice."

"What the kid is *really* asking," Putterman said with

more than a trace of exasperation, "is are we going to be in the line of fire?"

"Worried?"

"Damn right!" Putterman exclaimed. "People get killed all the time by stray bullets. Besides, we're responsible for these women."

"Somehow," Longarm said cryptically, "I don't think it's the prisoners that you're really worried about."

Putterman didn't like to hear that because it was the truth. Longarm said, "Why don't you just pull up at the livery and make arrangements for the team? They're going to need some rest."

"What are we supposed to do with the women and that Ortega fella, providing he's still alive?"

Longarm leaned far over and peered into the wagon. He could see Ortega lying stretched out on the floor and he was a real mess. The women had bloodied his face and Ortega's shirt and pants were torn open. Longarm didn't even want to think about what had happened to his prisoner because it might cause him to start feeling very guilty.

"All right," Longarm said a few minutes later when the wagon came to a stop. "I'll go arrest Marshal Haggerty and we can cram everyone in his two jail cells."

"That'll be cozy," Hawkins said.

"Very cozy," Longarm agreed, climbing down and checking his six-gun.

"If the marshal kills you first," Putterman called, "I'm not waiting around. I'll pull out for Colorado without you!"

"You do that," Longarm yelled back.

Longarm was aware of the attention that he was attracting as he strode down the boardwalk towards the marshal's office. It was almost as much attention as their caged prisoners were receiving.

When he came to the door of the office, Longarm drew his six-gun and took a deep breath. He placed his hand on the doorknob and started to open it and step inside, but suddenly he saw Marshal Haggerty's reflection in the front window and the man was moving awfully fast.

Longarm jumped aside, kicking the door open and flattening against the outside wall. A great blast of shot filled the doorway, shredding its frame. Longarm stuck his gun around the frame and fired once. The shotgun boomed a second time and Longarm dropped to his belly, scooted into the doorway, and fired again. His first two shots had been merely to distract, for he had not yet located his target. But now he saw the big marshal hauling his gun up to fire.

"Freeze!" Longarm shouted.

"Like hell!" Haggerty bellowed, as his gun thundered in his meaty fist.

But Longarm had already rolled and fired all in the same motion, and his bullet ripped into Haggerty's gut right over his belt buckle. The man's feet jittered on the floor and Longarm shot him again, this time through the chest. Haggerty's eyes rolled up into his head. His feet stopped dancing and he stumbled back until he struck his jail cell bars. Then, he twisted as if he were trying to run and hide, and held himself erect against the bars of his cell.

Longarm came to his feet and stepped inside the office, watching Haggerty hang onto the bars and then begin to slide to the floor.

"Dammit, Haggerty," Longarm complained, "it makes me sick when a lawman goes bad. Hurts every one of us who tries to live up to the law. Do you understand what I'm telling you?"

Haggerty's forehead thunked hard against the jail cell, so hard that the bars rattled, and then he sighed and collapsed.

Longarm punched the expended shells from his six-gun and went over to the marshal's body. He extracted the cell keys from the man's pocket and opened both cells in preparation for receiving their wagonload of prisoners.

"Better not put you in one," Longarm mused aloud to the marshal. "Better to drag you outside for the undertaker."

And that's what Longarm did. He dragged the heavy marshal outside and a little ways up the street, then laid him out, saying to a gaping spectator, "Go get the undertaker."

"Yes, sir!"

Longarm paused to catch his breath. The marshal must have weighed a quarter of a ton. Longarm became aware of the big staring crowd, and he supposed that he owed them a brief explanation. If for no other reason, then so that Lucy would no longer be under suspicion.

Longarm spoke very loudly although this aggravated his still-aching throat. "Folks," he began, "I'm a U.S. deputy marshal, and the sad truth of the matter is that your own marshal was in cahoots with Juan Ortega, Manuel Padilla, Renaldo Lopez, and Hal Brodie. They all plotted and took part in the murder of Don Luis Ortega."

Longarm paused to let them absorb this startling news, then continued his explanation. "The important thing that you need to understand is that Mrs. Ortega had nothing to do with her husband's death. The only one of the killers still alive is Ortega, and he's going to rot in Yuma Prison."

The crowd stared, and Longarm batted dust from his

clothes. "So now that you all know what happened, why don't you all just go on about your business? Your undertaker has got work to do and you folks need to hire a new marshal."

"How about you?" a man dressed in a fine black suit called. "We'd pay you even better than the federal government."

"No, thanks," Longarm said. "I got three weeks of paid vacation coming when I deliver those female prisoners to Denver, Colorado."

"You'd be better off staying here," the man dared to argue. "But we respect your decision and we'll find an *honest* lawman this time."

"Good," Longarm said, heading back up the street to tell Putterman to unload the Yuma Prison girls and whatever they'd left of Juan Ortega.

LONGARM

Explore the exciting Old West with
one of the men who made it wild!